D0877752

Jill La Forge Jones

FREEDOM'S EDGE

An American Trilogy

*A Story of America's War for Independence in the South:
The People Who Fought and Won, and Those Who Fought and Lost*

Jill LaForge Jones

Book Two
SURVIVING THE NOW

Also by the Author

_____

Written as Jill Jones:
Emily's Secret
My Lady Caroline
The Scottish Rose
Essence of My Desire (retitled A Scent of Magic)
Circle of the Lily
The Island
Bloodline
Remember Your Lies
Every Move You Make

_____

Written as Emily LaForge:
Beneath the Ravens' Moon
Shadow Haven

AUTHOR BIO

Jill LaForge Jones is the award-winning author of eleven novels of romance and suspense. She holds a bachelor's degree in Journalism with emphasis on Professional Writing from the University of Oklahoma where she graduated Magna Cum Laude and was inducted into Phi Beta Kappa. She has written for a wide variety of audiences and media, including print, audio, video, and online content. During the last twenty years, she served as director of the Swannanoa Valley Museum in Black Mountain, NC, and director of Marketing & Communications for the Blue Ridge National Heritage Area, work in which she traveled throughout the region and learned about the unique history and culture of western North Carolina.

This is a work of fiction. Although some characters are historical figures, and some incidents are true to history, other names, characters, places, and incidents are either the product of the author's imagination or used fictitiously.

ISBN– 9780967697253 Paperback
ISBN– 9780967697260 Epub

Cover and book design by Russell Shuler.

AUTHOR'S NOTE

When I was growing up, the history taught in school about America's war for independence was generally depicted through a lens of northern action—the Boston Tea Party, Lexington and Concord, Paul Revere's midnight ride, creation of the Declaration of Independence in Philadelphia, George Washington and Valley Forge, etc. As a student, I was given the impression that the whole thing was relatively simple, based on the "taxation without representation" issue, freedom of religion, and the desire of early immigrants for affordable land.

While all this is true, the picture is far more complex, and it leaves out entire cultures of the natives of the land who were not only disenfranchised by the white man's encroachment, but also came perilously close to extinction. It leaves out the story of the immigrants who forged their new lives in the South—primarily South and North Carolina—and who played a significant role in the eventual defeat of Cornwallis. And it fails to depict the complexity of the relations between white and red man, between a culture with superior technology and one still in the stone age (think guns vs. bow and arrow, steel knives vs. stone spear points.) The story fails to show how over time, the natives' desire to own that technology, partly in self-defense, and to trade with the British for their weapons, manufactured goods, and even trinkets led them to concede land through treaties that many times were ignored or broken. In spite of this, the Cherokee were allies of the British in the War for Independence, and as such met defeat as well.

As a twenty-first century white female, it is difficult to imagine life on this southern frontier between 1750-1780. Who were these immigrants who came into places like Charleston and Wilmington rather than the more typical points of entry such as Philadelphia and New York? Why did they come? What were they running to? Or from? Did they come of their own accord, or were they indentured or enslaved? How bad was life where they came from that they would risk everything and face the unknown in a land rich with promise but rife with danger?

And what of those who already lived on that land? Natives whose ancestors had been there for thousands of years? What did they make of these newcomers? And what part did they play in the white man's war for independence?

Immigration and the problems inherent in the process have been part of the history of mankind since the beginning of time: One tribe wants the land of another, and so will take it by force or cunning. Or one tribe builds a wall to keep another tribe from entering its land. Or tribes unite through marriage or treaty only to fall apart again through treachery or betrayal. It is a never-ending saga of humankind.

My quest is not to resolve this eternal issue, but rather through this work of historical fiction provide the reader with insight into the incredible complexities that faced both the immigrants who came into the southern ports of the British colonies in the mid-eighteenth century and the natives already upon these shores. I have tried to remain true to historic dates and figures, but this is fiction, life imagined in a time and place over two and a half centuries ago, and history sometimes gets fuzzy—in my research, I sometimes encountered different versions of events, times, and places. I have chosen the ones that best fit my story.

My "tribes" are primarily the British, Irish, Highland Scots, Africans, and the Cherokee, descendants of all of which can be found in the mountains and valleys of western North and South Carolina and northern Georgia today. Other "contributing tribes" include the French, Moravians, Scots-Irish, Germans, Swiss, and the Catawba, Shawnee and Creek Indians. The mountains and foothills of North and South Carolina became home to a stew of humanity from both sides of the Atlantic and both hemispheres, brought together by hope, despair, fear, greed, desire for power, lust for land, and that ultimate and elusive aspiration, freedom.

This trilogy is dedicated to those keepers of history in small museums throughout our country, specifically those in western North Carolina, and to the Blue Ridge National Heritage Area.

CHAPTER ONE

On board the *Orion*, April 1746

"*Run for your life, Will! They've got us!*" *The words crashed into his ears, along with the sound of guns, the cries of men dying. Sleeting rain pelted his face, and he wanted to run, but he didn't know which way to go. A horrid, metallic smell began to pervade the battlefield, the smell of blood mixed with the stench of gunpowder.*

"*Run for your life!*" *he heard again and realized it was his friend Duncan who was calling to him. He turned just in time to see Duncan's head blown away. One minute his friend was alive and warning him, the next he was like a piece of raw meat crumpling to the ground.*

"*Run!*" *he thought he heard again, but it couldn't be Duncan. Duncan was dead.*

Will tried to run, but his feet were mired in the soggy ground of Culloden Muir. He stumbled and fell headlong into the muck. He tried to breathe but was suffocated by the watery ground that oozed around him, even into his nose. He tried to see, but all was suddenly turning dark.

Around him, the screams of the dying filled his ears. He closed his eyes tight, held his breath, clenched his fists, and waited for a bullet or the killing stab of a British bayonet.

Will awoke with a start, bathed in a cold sweat. Would that nightmare ever leave him, the memory of that massacre on the Culloden battlefield that had destroyed his life? Taken his family, his entire clan? He sat up and felt his body being gently rocked in the small bunk where he had slept and remembered where he was...on board a sailing ship, headed away from Scotland and all that he'd ever known.

He rolled over in his tiny bunk, trying to fall asleep again, but his tormented thoughts wouldn't leave him. He remembered regaining consciousness on the sodden moor, how silent it was. The icy rain had stopped. The sky was dark. It was night, and he was alive. He managed to drag himself to his feet and looked around, expecting to see redcoats, but no one was in sight. Shivering, his mind numb, he slogged away from the killing field, not knowing here he was going, only that he had to get away from this place.

Now, as he lay in the dark, remembering that evil day, anger overcame grief, as it always did. He and his Da and all his kinsmen had fought alongside the man who owned their farm, and their lives, Lord Lewis Gordon. But for what? For a royal person he had hardly heard of who some thought should be the English king. Bonnie Prince Charlie, they'd called him. What kind of king had a name like that? And why did Will's kin and clansmen have to die for him? They were Scots, not Englishmen. Will knew his Da was dead, they were all dead. He would be dead too except for the kindness and courage of the couple who'd rescued him in Inverness.

Knowing he could never return to his mother and sisters, or their farm, where redcoats would be watching and would as soon hang him as not, he'd made his way down the mountain to Inverness, taking shelter in an old warehouse. Starving and exhausted, he'd lain across a bundle of shipping sacks, and unable to fight it any longer, fell asleep. A deep voice had startled him awake, and Ian Brodie, another Highlander who hated the British, had taken him home and later arranged passage out of Scotland aboard the *Orion*, the ship that sheltered him now. The captain, John Taylor, had been kind enough as well, but he'd made clear from the outset that Will was to earn his keep like any other of the sailors, despite his young age.

The *Orion* plied the Atlantic between Scotland and America, and much of the westbound cargo included immigrants eager to taste the freedom and prosperity they'd heard would be theirs in the New World. They were to board just such a group at their next port of call on the Isle of Skye, where Captain Taylor's client, Fergus McKinney, tacksman for the Laird of Clan McKinnon, had booked passage for as many of his tenants as wanted to leave. "He told me they're leaving the place before it all turns to shambles," Taylor had shared with Will. "The Laird's already left for London, wanting no part of this current political business, and the tenants canna afford the rents still demanded by the Laird." He paused a moment, then added, "He's a good man, McKinney."

Paid shipping for most of 'em. I just hope what the man's heard about America is true. Seems like a wild, unsettled land t' me."

A wild, unsettled land. Will decided that could be no worse than the wild, dangerous land he was leaving behind.

Captain Taylor introduced Will to his sailmaster, Mr. Simpson, as the new ship's boy. "See that he stays busy."

Simpson scowled. "I ain't no babysitter."

Will took offense at being treated like a child. He was almost grown, would be thirteen come summer. "I ain't no baby," he retorted. "Just tell me what you want of me, and you'll have it."

Captain Taylor raised his eyebrows in amusement and gave Simpson a look that brooked no further argument. "You've been grousin' about not havin' enough help," he said. "Well, sir, now you have it." And with that, he turned and left.

Will heard Simpson swear beneath his breath. He waited for some kind of direction from him, but the man remained silent, concentrating on his job of guiding the ship out of the harbor and into the river that led to the open sea. The captain hadn't given him any specific orders, but wanting to carry his load, Will looked around the deck and saw large ropes lying about in disarray. Without waiting for orders, he sat on the deck and began to neaten the mess, coiling the heavy lines and clearing safe space for passage. A deckhand passing by commented, "Aye, good job, mate!" at which Simpson looked over and saw what Will had done.

"Guess that's as good a chore for a boy as any," he uttered.

Will gritted his teeth. "I can do more. Just say what," he called back, trying not to sound petulant. But Simpson ignored him.

The late April wind was brisk and chill, and Will shivered beneath his light woolen jacket. As his shock dissipated, he began to realize the enormity of the change his life had taken since the horror on Culloden Moor: his Da and others dead, probably his whole family, and him here on a sailing ship leaving Scotland! His heart was so heavy it felt as if it would bleed from his chest, but at the same time, his mind and upbringing by his stoic father told him to buck up and look toward the morrow.

To what, he didn't know.

CHAPTER TWO

On the voyage from Inverness to the Isle of Skye, Will followed Simpson around, trying to both guess the man's needs while trying to stay out of his way, feeling very much like a trained dog. As sailing master, Simpson was in charge of navigation and sailing. He'd learned that Simpson, although dour, was respected by the crew, that he preferred coffee to tea, chewed tobacco from America, and liked his grog. Overall, Will decided, he wasn't so bad. Just grumpy.

When the *Orion* reached the Isle of Skye, Will made haste to help with assisting the passengers as they came aboard. Since there was no quay or wharf in the small town, the ship rode at anchor, and the passengers and their belongings were shuttled from land by tenders. The people arrived first, and Will saw the anxiety and fatigue on their faces as he helped them onto the ship's deck. But they were also happy and relieved that at last they were on their way to a life they expected would hold more for them than the one they were leaving behind.

The baggage was more difficult to bring aboard than the people. Some of the travelers had heavy trunks and crates that had to be lifted from the tender that rocked on the surface of the water up to the heights of the deck of the rolling ship. Although he was only twelve, Will had apprenticed with his Da for nearly two years as a blacksmith and farrier for Lord Gordon, and his muscles were strong and able.

Once all the travelers and their goods were on board, Captain Taylor shook hands with a large man, Fergus McKinney, Will reckoned. The captain welcomed them and gave them a cursory tour of the ship before showing them the quarters they would all share for the next several weeks. "Will, please help these good folks settle in, then report back to me," he said, indicating for Will to help the passengers down the companionway to the steerage area.

"Aye, aye, sir," Will said with just a tinge of pride. Maybe they were no longer going to consider him a boy. He explained to the group that the *Orion* had no private passenger quarters, that all would share the space belowdecks, at which some of the women tittered in distress. He wasn't sure how to overcome this but knew he must make these people as comfortable as possible. The captain had made it his duty.

"Come along, let me show you," he said, descending the steep stairway. He helped each person safely down, and when they were all gathered, he said with forced cheer, "Those there are the bunks," and indicated the shelf-like structures along the ship's wall. "Feel free to choose one for yourselves." Again, there was grumbling all around.

"I'm having a word with the captain, "McKinney said, and others nodded. "I didn't realize the quarters would be so limited."

Will froze for a moment. He couldn't let the captain think he was inept at this, his first real assignment on board. "Wait!" he said, thinking quickly. "The captain is very busy. Perhaps we can sort this out ourselves."

McKinney eyed Will quizzically. "What have you in mind, boy?"

Will took in a deep breath and blew it out, raising the dark auburn hair that lay above his brows. "Of course, sir, you are welcome to take it up with the captain, but the fact is, this is the only living space on the ship provided for passengers. The only other quarters hold the crew and officers in whose care you have placed your well-being on this journey." He hesitated before he dared to continue. He had no idea if Captain Taylor would approve of what he was going to say, because after all, Taylor had been paid to take these people to America. But he forged on: "Your only option is for those who do not wish to lodge here for the voyage to return to shore."

At this, the people grew quiet. "Let us pray," McKinney said suddenly, and as Will watched, they all joined hands in a circle, bowed their heads, and were silent. Only McKinney spoke. He prayed for guidance in this decision, and then he too grew quiet. Will guessed he was listening for an answer from the Lord, which he must have received, for in his next supplication, he prayed for a safe journey. Then he directed the immigrants to select their bunks and implored them to be kind to one another. "My family will hold back until all others are settled," he told Will.

Relieved that no one had opted to leave the ship, Will left them to sort it out, but when he returned an hour later, he found a woman in tears, wailing at her husband. "I knew we should not have come, Mr. McKinney," she cried. "This is abominable. There isn't even room for us to share a bed."

Mr. McKinney looked around and saw the others looking on in interest. Will wondered what kind of man would let his wife speak so to him in public? But McKinney only took his wife in his arms and comforted her. "Now, Esther, we made this plan together, you and I. You and the girls can have the bunk. I'll find a place to nest. 'Tis only for a short time, remember. And when we're safely on the other shore, you'll be glad of it."

Will quickly came up with a way to resolve Mrs. McKinney's despair, or at least assuage it somewhat. "Sir," he said, approaching the older man, who seemed in age much like that of his Da. "I have found an extra bunk for your family. Here," he said, pointing to his own meagre sleeping quarters. "This one is free. 'Tis the last one, I believe, so if you'll have it, 'tis yours."

Will's bunk was not far from the other one that the McKinney's had claimed, and Fergus McKinney quickly took him up on the offer, not knowing Will was sacrificing his own space. A girl not much younger than Will left Mrs. McKinney's side and ran to him. "Oh, thank you! We shall be fine, I am certain. Mam's just all nerves over this journey, you know."

She wasn't the only one, Will thought grimly. His nerves had been fraught for many days as he made his escape and found asylum on board the *Orion*. "Aye. 'Tis good that we can work this out." He wasn't sure where he would sleep, but better the passengers be happy than cause the captain any trouble.

"My name's Margaret," the girl said, boldly extending her hand. "What's yours?"

Will blushed. He'd rarely spoken to a girl, not a stranger at any rate. Still, he took her hand. "Will," he said. "Will Gordon."

"Margaret! You mustn't bother him," Mrs. McKinney chastised her daughter.

But Fergus McKinney just gave a hearty laugh, and Will liked him instantly. "Leave her alone, Esther," McKinney said. "You know she's not one to hang back. 'Tis good for her to make friends. It'll be a better trip for it." Then he turned to Will. "From your speech, I ken you're a Highlander. From where do you hail, lad?"

Will bristled, but he supposed he must get used to being called a lad until his body caught up with his estimation of his manhood. "Come from the land of Lord Lewis Gordon, sir, near Elgin."

McKinney's brow furrowed. "Don't know much about that part of the Highlands, but seems to me like it must be somewhere near Culloden. You hear anything about that bad business up there on that moor?"

Will felt his ears grow warm, and when he looked around, he could see that all within hearing distance were listening to this exchange. Word had travelled fast through the Highlands, it seemed. He hesitated, looked down at his hands, then straightened and looked McKinney in the eye. With great difficulty, he replied, "Aye, sir. I was there."

At that, a low murmur rustled through the group. Fergus McKinney's face fell. "I'm sorry, son. Was it as bloody as we've heard tell?"

Will did not want to talk about what he'd seen or heard. "Aye," he said again brusquely. "Excuse me. I must report to the captain." And with that, he dashed up the companionway and onto the quarterdeck where Captain Taylor was overseeing the readying of the ship for the final leg of their voyage—across the Atlantic.

Chapter Three

The crew had hoisted the anchor and set the sails, and the huge vessel began to move out to open water. "All steady below?" the captain asked him.

"I believe so, sir, although they are very nervous."

"Can't say as I blame 'em. I'm always nervous myself until we're underway." Taylor gave a small laugh, an uneasy laugh it seemed to Will, and he found it neither amusing nor comforting.

Will turned to Simpson. "I'm at your service, sir. Next duty?"

"Just stay out of my way," Simpson growled. "Go to th' fo'c's'le and see if you can help the cookie. That old idler's got many a more mouth t' feed now. Just don't get in his way either."

Glad to have something to busy his hands, Will made his way forward to the ship's galley, where the "old idler," Ben Shepherd, and two other hands were in their constant state of preparing food. "Ben, sir, I'm told to help you out."

Ben was a man of few words. He'd lost a leg in an accident during a storm, and so was unfit for deck duty or to stand watch. Thus his designation by Simpson as an "idler." Will knew for a fact Ben and his fellows in the galley were far from idle. He'd been asked to help them before, and he saw first-hand what it took to feed a large crew. And now...their many passengers would be added to their work.

Not answering Will directly, Ben turned to one of the other men and indicated for them to pass a large bag over to him, which he handed in turn to Will. He gave Will a knife and a large bowl. "On deck. Peel," was all he said.

Will found a niche between a couple of large barrels that were lashed to the deck and settled down to his chore. The day was blustery, and looking up, he saw the white sails stretched to their fullest against a thinly clouded sky. He felt the ship moving with a silent might and was awed by the power of the wind and the waters. They were sailing south from the Isle of Skye on what Simpson had told him was called "Little Minch," an extension of the Minch waterway that separated the Highlands from the Outer Hebrides. All this was new to him, and in many ways, fascinating, although at times, also daunting. He had thought about becoming a sailor when he got older, but the constant motion made him ill at ease, and he reckoned he was better off on land.

The only problem, he contemplated as he peeled potato after potato and plonked them into the tepid sea water in the bowl, was there to be any place for him in this new land to which they were bound? He was an orphan now, and penniless, but he had a trade. Perhaps he could find work as a blacksmith when they arrived. And then it occurred to him, he wasn't exactly sure of where they were going, other than to America, someplace Captain Taylor considered to be a "wild and unsettled place."

Lost in his reverie, he didn't see the girl approach him until she sat down beside him. Startled, he almost spilled the bowl of newly peeled potatoes overboard.

"Margaret!" he exclaimed, remembering her name. "Does your Da know you are out here?"

Margaret had eyes the color of a cloudless summer sky that sparkled as brightly as the glints of sunshine on the ocean waves. Her hair was fair, with curls that tossed playfully in the ocean breeze.

"He does not," she said, grinning mischievously. "There's so many folks below he'll not miss me for a time. Mam is so distraught she's taken to the bed for a time. And sister Mary, well, she's of no use. A shy little crybaby, that's what she is. Probably clinging to Mam's skirt taking a nap."

Will wasn't sure what to do, but he still had a mountain of potatoes to peel, and this girl wasn't really his problem, although he did wonder what McKinney would do if he found her with him. "Why'd you come here?" he asked a bit gruffly. He didn't want to get into trouble.

"Here? On the ship, you mean?"

"No. Here. Where I'm sitting."

She laughed, and Will found the sound musical to his ears. "Silly. I'm bored down there. I wasn't really looking for you, but then, I found you! My good luck."

Will's ears reddened again; he could feel them burning. "It's not safe for a girl like you up here. You'd best go back to your family."

"I get sea sick down below."

"Oh." Will had experienced that problem himself, and he knew it was no fun. "You'll get used to the motion," he assured her in his most manly of tones.

"Are you a sailor?"

Will considered his answer carefully. He didn't want to admit he was a mere ship's boy, an errand runner for the captain and Simpson. "Maybe. I'm learning the ropes."

"It looks dangerous to me."

"It is. I've been told many a sailor has fallen to his watery grave from up there," he said, pointing his knife toward the tall masts.

"You must be very brave. Da told me after you left all about that battle at Culloden. How brave you are to have fought there, and how lucky not to have died." When Will did not reply, she pressed on. "What was it like, all that shooting and ruckus?"

Tears sprang unbidden to Will's eyes, and he blinked furiously, not wanting her to see. "I...I don't want to talk about it. Please," was all he could manage.

They sat together in silence, Will peeling furiously, Margaret gazing up at the sky and the clouds and the billowing white sails. "Mam is afraid, but I'm not," she revealed suddenly. "There was nothing left for us in Scotland, at least that's what Da told us."

"That's what some of those folks below told me when they came aboard," Will said, glad for the change in subject. "Funny. They're anxious to be leaving the land of their birth, but they're going to a land that is unknown to them."

"'Tis not entirely unknown," Margaret said. "We've had letters from friends who've gone there. They say there's land aplenty for everyone. A new life!"

"Where did your friends go?" Will wanted to know.

"A place called North Carolina. I hear it's hot there. I'll be glad to be warm for a change. Scotland's always so cold." Then she paused and frowned. "I wonder if there are Indians there."

* * *

"Wilmington," Simpson said when Will brought his dinner to his cabin later that day and inquired of their destination.

"Not New York or Philadelphia?" Will had heard of these ports but never of Wilmington. Actually, he'd heard very little of North Carolina. "Where is it?"

"South." Simpson seemed to have softened towards Will since that first day. Will had worked hard to earn his keep—and the respect of this man and the captain. "Here. Take a look."

Simpson unrolled a parchment map and spread it out on his navigation table, anchoring the corners with various weights. "We're here," he said, pointing to a spot in the upper right-hand portion of the map. "Here's Skye. Here's our current course," he drew an imaginary line with his right forefinger down the length of the channel. Then he placed the fingers of his left hand in the lower left quadrant of the map. "And here's where we're going. Wilmington. On the Cape Fear River, on the very south end of North Carolina."

Will's eyes followed Simpson's finger as the sailing master continued, "And here's how we're gettin' there." Simpson traced a course between the two. "God willin'," he added. "The sea's a flirty lady, boy, capricious and unpredictable, as is the weather. 'Tis my job, and my determination, to make the crossing as quickly as possible, before the storms of summer."

"How long will it take us, sir?"

"Depends. Six weeks at the minimum. Could be nine. If we get blown off course, could be long as twelve or more. That'd be a real problem, tryin' t' feed that bunch. There's nowhere to stop out here on the blue to bring on vittles."

Will's gaze wandered up the outline of the coast, and he spotted the places he'd heard of. "May I ask, sir, why we're not going here?" he pointed to New York. "Or here?" indicating Boston, "or here?" pointing to Philadelphia.

"Too many people there for the likes of these Highlanders," Simpson replied, turning to the business of eating his supper. "And no cheap land left to be had. Lots have already gone to North Carolina instead. Clannish as they are, they're stickin' together. Still speakin' th' old language, movin' as families and villages, as you've seen with this bunch."

Will poured Simpson a generous portion of grog, the watered-down rum that seemed in plentiful supply aboard the *Orion*. "Will there, uh, be English there, sir?"

At that, Simpson let out a low laugh, but one that didn't quite make it to his eyes. "North Carolina is a British Royal Colony," he said, taking a swig of the drink. "Of course, there's English."

"Do they hate Scots Highlanders there?" Will suddenly feared maybe he'd cross the ocean only to find himself again at the mercy of the murdering English.

Simpson eyed him thoughtfully. "I know what happened to you back there at Culloden, Will. The captain told me. But that doesn't mean all English are bad, or that they hate the Scots. They were trying to roust the Pretender and keep the throne in King George's hands. It was about power, pure and simple. It was war, and war ain't pretty."

Will left Simpson, promising to return later to retrieve his dish and cup. His mind was racing. North Carolina! Wilmington! He'd found some comfort in learning that he'd be with his own people, those who spoke the old language, Gaelic, and whose ways he knew. He returned to steerage to check on the passengers. The captain had assigned four other 'idlers' to serve meals to the passengers for the duration of the journey, and they had delivered to them buckets of the burgoo in which Will's peeled potatoes resided with bits of mutton and turnips. Will mingled among the travelers, casually looking for Margaret, but also on the lookout for complaints or unmet needs. The meal seemed to have assuaged their earlier grumbling, and a number of them were preparing to bed down for the night.

McKinney, however, was not one of them. A big, robust man with a ready smile, he produced a battered fiddle from his kit and struck a chord, which got everyone's attention. "We have us a long voyage ahead, friends," he said, "might as well have some fun along the way." And with that, he set about making his bow fly across the strings, and his daughter, Margaret, immediately started to dance. Will watched, enchanted by this spritely girl, and afraid of her at the same time.

She turned in circles, then took the hand of one of her young cousins, and those gathered around parted to make room for their dancing. As Will watched, Margaret and her cousin separated, then grabbed hands with two others in the crowd, drawing them into the circle of dance. On it went, each dancer inviting another to join in until almost all in that narrow space were dancing to McKinney's fiddle tunes. There wasn't room for much circling as more dancers came onto the floor, but they made do by step dancing almost in place.

Will was startled when he felt a hand take his, and he found himself being pulled into the dance by Margaret. "I...I can't," he started to protest. "Don't know how."

"Oh, c'mon. Nothing to it. Just move your feet in time to the music." She raised her skirt to show her feet. "See. 'Tis easy! C'mon. Try it!"

Will's face turned crimson at the sight of her ankles, and he quickly looked away. But he allowed her to bring him into the midst of the merriment, and he soon found it was, as she'd said, easy. And oddly, it lifted his spirits for the first time since leaving his home on the high moors.

When the music came to an end, Margaret explained to Will that this was what they called the 'American dance.' "It's how we encouraged our families and villagers to join us in going to America," she said. "Da and Mam had already made up their minds we should leave, but Mary and I feared we would be lonely leaving all those we knew behind. So one night, Da summoned everybody to the town center, and he announced our plans to move to America, giving his reasons that they all knew well enough. Seems there was not much future left for us there. Then he invited others to come with us, and then he played this fiddle tune. 'Come with us, countrymen!' he called. 'Join in the dance and come to America with us!' And before nightfall, most all had decided to come with us."

Margaret looked at the other passengers who were now serious about bedding down in the straw-filled bunks. "I just hope they don't regret it and blame us for making a choice urged on by Da."

Will took his leave and made his way back onto the deck, welcoming the fresh night air after the stuffy quarters below made worse by the heat of the dancing. But he had to admit, it had been fun, and Margaret, well, she was something!

He reported the musical evening to Captain Taylor, who was pleased. "I'm glad this McKinney fellow is a fiddler," Taylor said. "No one on our crew plays music, and I had no time to recruit a musician in Inverness, leaving suddenly like we did."

Will didn't understand. "Recruit a musician?"

"Aye, son. I like always to have a musician on board these passages. Tomorrow, and all days the weather will allow, I'll ask you t' bring 'em up on deck for a lively dance and maybe even some singing. Keeps 'em happy, and they can get some fresh air and exercise to boot."

Having given up his own berth below, Will left the captain and sought a place to lay his head. He ended up nestling inside a large coil of rope on deck, and before drifting off to sleep, he looked up into a clear night sky and saw what seemed like a million stars, twinkling lights that that were reflected faintly on the ocean's waves. It gave him hope for a swift journey, and an odd but much needed sense of peace.

If only the dream he'd come to dread, the dream that had visited nightly since that terrible afternoon on Culloden Moor, would leave him tonight, not to return. But it was not to be. Sometime in the darkness, Will cried out in terror, and the sailor who was on watch heard him. Several hands found him and shook him awake. "Are you all right, boy?" one of them said. Will looked into their anxious faces and was embarrassed.

"Yes. Bad dream's all." But the sailors seemed to know what demons haunted him, and they found him a berth in their quarters, and for the rest of the journey they heard his cries but said nothing of them to him in the morning.

CHAPTER FOUR

Thus the voyage began, with fair winds driving the big ship over what some of the sailors called the Sea of Green Darkness, what others called the Western Ocean. Will was kept busy, running messages from various stations to keep the captain and Mr. Simpson apprised of conditions on board, helping out the idlers in the galley, and attempting to make sure the passengers were as comfortable as possible. Which wasn't an easy task.

The steerage section of the ship was barely adequate to hold the number of voyagers Captain Taylor had taken aboard. As the days turned into weeks, the crowded conditions created frequent quarrels and confrontations, even among friends. The quality of their early meals lessened daily, as their fresh food supply grew stale, and Ben by necessity had to begin using staples such as the hard biscuits and dried meat that were more stable for a long ocean journey. Their water supply had dwindled, and all were now drinking beer, even the children.

The one thing that cheered them, besides the fair weather, was the music. As the captain had ordered, Will spoke with Mr. McKinney, who agreed to play for a daily afternoon dance on the quarterdeck. Even sailors who were off duty joined in, and after the dancing ceased, members of the crew often picked up singing from their posts. Theirs were songs of the sea, some of them sad, some silly, some frightening. Eventually many of the passengers learned the words and sang along, which helped pass the tedious time.

A few weeks into the voyage, Mother Nature showed her capricious spirit, which Will thought did not at all fit Simpson's description of 'flirty.' She turned downright mean.

The storm hit at daybreak, suddenly and with gale force winds that knocked the vessel about upon huge waves as if it were a toy boat. The passengers were terrified, and the captain ordered Will below. "Stay with them and keep them calm if you can. We're in for a blow, and I don't want to lose any of 'em overboard, so don't under any circumstances let any of 'em come up."

Although some of the passengers had suffered from sea sickness almost from the beginning, the hammering of the waves sent many more to their buckets, and the stench became nearly unbearable. No breakfast could be served, and as the storm wore on, hunger set in, especially for the younger children. Women cried in fear at the creaking and groaning of the planks, and one older man took to praying. All were often thrown off their balance and many fell to the floor as the angle of the planks beneath them shifted sharply from the force of the waves. Will himself felt ill but was loathe to show weakness, so he sought out Mr. McKinney.

"Don't suppose you could play us a tune, sir," he asked, thinking it highly unlikely. But the good man only grinned. "If I can get myself propped so's my hands are free, I'll give it a try," he offered. With that, he managed to make his way to his small berth beneath which lay a bag that Will knew contained the instrument. Then sitting on the floor, he wedged his substantial body between the upright post that supported the sleeping bunks and the heavy table that was secured to the floor with large bolts. And he began to play.

It was not a dance tune this time. It was a traditional Scottish tune which everyone recognized, and the melody brought a hush over the travelers, for the moment calming the chaos. Some of the people followed McKinney's lead and settled themselves as best they could on the floor, which prevented them from falling, although they had to hold on to keep from sliding across the damp surface as the ship dipped and swayed. Many of the women and children tried to steady themselves within the confines of their small berths. But all grew quieter in spite of the storm, and someone began to sing. Oddly, during this time, it seemed to Will that the wind let up some as well, as if it, too, was calmed by their singing.

"I'm glad we didn't die," Margaret told Will the following day. "There for a while, I thought we'd never see the shores of America."

"We're not there yet," Will said, not wanting her to think this was the only storm they might encounter. And indeed, it wasn't.

Two more storms, a food shortage, short tempers, illnesses among the passengers, two deaths, and seven weeks later, the lookout called "Land ho!" from high in the crow's nest, and cheers arose from those gathered for the afternoon music on deck.

"Praise God," Esther McKinney uttered, clutching little Mary to her side. Will and Margaret were close enough to hear her, and Will added, "and praise Captain Taylor and Mr. Simpson, and all the crew who have brought us through!" At this, the passengers gave a loud 'huzzah!' Will looked over at Esther and saw she was not happy that he'd given credit to mere mortals for a safe journey.

Will saw Simpson beckon him, and he ran to get his latest instructions. "We reckon this is the inlet to Cape Fear," Simpson told him, "but we're not out of danger yet. 'Tis not a harbor like is found in Charlestown and Philadelphia. 'Tis but the entrance to a river, and from experience, I know it has shoals we must avoid. Last thing we need now is to go aground. I'm going to hove-to when we get closer, and I'll have you, Clemson, Turk, and Bono launch the tenders and take soundings to make sure we know where the sandbars are. I'll also be watching the tides. With luck, we can move on upriver at the next high tide."

Will was astonished that Simpson would trust him with such an important mission, but he readily said, "Aye," and the plans were laid. By the time the *Orion* came close enough, the sun was setting, and Captain Taylor postponed the exploration until morning. The ocean was too deep to drop an anchor, so Simpson set the sails to hold the ship in place as much as possible for the night, making no progress in any direction.

Ben raided the slim remainder of the ship's stores for the evening meal, one all hoped would be their last on board. Their respite from sailing allowed the crew members to put a line in the water, and Ben was happy to serve up fresh-caught fish fried in the last of the lard on hand.

Will was among the last to be served, and he took his plate and fork and settled into a nook on the deck he'd frequented on the journey, a quiet corner where he fought his demons unobserved. He'd barely sat down when Margaret appeared at his side.

"What will you do once we get on land?" she asked without preamble.

It was an issue Will had considered often on the journey, and his answer was simple. "I don't know."

"Do you have kin or friends in North Carolina?"

"No." A knot tied itself in his throat. He had no kin anymore, and no friends except those he'd made on the voyage.

"So why don't you come with us? Da says we're going up country along the river, see what land's available. Says there's others of us Highlanders there."

Will was flattered that she'd thought about him in this way, but he doubted she spoke for her Da. "I...I don't know. I guess I'll see what comes my way in Wilmington."

"Are you a farmer?" she pressed. "Da would need a good hand when we settle."

"Was once. And a farrier. Can build a good horseshoe in a smithy." He stabbed at his fish, now cold in his tin plate. "Wonder if there's any work to be had as a blacksmith over here?"

Margaret's expression turned glum. "I'd think you'd like to find some land of your own in time," she mused. "You're young for it now, but soon you might apply for your own land grant."

Will was taken aback at Margaret's apparent knowledge of how things worked in America. She was very smart. Smarter than he considered himself to be. "I hadn't thought of that," he admitted. He didn't admit that he didn't know what a land grant was and made a mental note to ask Mr. McKinney about this in private.

The following morning when the sun was at an angle where they could see the sounding lines as they sank into the ocean waters, Will and the others set out in two tenders, rowing toward shore and dragging a line behind each at a depth needed for the *Orion* to make passageway into the river. Several times the lines snagged and bumped over the bottom the closer to land they came, but each time they were able to maneuver to a deeper place. It took several hours, but they were able to discern a deep-water entry, which they marked on either side with long sticks flying small white flags.

It was mid-afternoon when they returned to the ship, exhausted and thirsty. They reported their work to Simpson, who conferred with the captain, and it was decided to move ahead at once, as the tide was in their favor at the moment.

"Hold your breath, Will Gordon," Mr. Simpson said, "and pray your markings are true. Otherwise, we'll be in a real pickle if we land on a sandbar."

Will did hold his breath, more than once, as Simpson and his crew eased the heavy ship around the shoals and between the markers they'd set. He jumped when he felt a bump and the ship hesitated, but Simpson managed to press on through until they passed a big island to their starboard, a navigational guide that let the sailing master know they'd made the crossing successfully.

Captain Taylor called Will and the other three who'd set the markers to join him on the quarterdeck. "Well done, men," he said. Men! The captain had called them men. It was obvious the others were older than he, and seasoned sailors. But he'd included Will in that term, and for his part, Will chose to believe that he'd made his own crossing—from boy to man.

CHAPTER FIVE

The Cape Fear River, Simpson told Will, was navigable for twenty miles inland. The present Governor of North Carolina, Gabriel Johnston, had favored the more inland location of Wilmington over the Port of Brunswick, which had been established by the Moore family, who had become Johnston's rivals. "McKinney's paid us to go up to Wilmington. Says it'll make their journey into the back country shorter."

Will climbed to a high point at the bow of the ship, keeping watch into the water, ready to signal a course adjustment if necessary to keep the ship aligned with the deeper water of the river. When they bypassed the Port of Brunswick, he heard the disappointment some of the passengers expressed at being so close to land but unable to put their feet at last on solid ground.

By evening, however, the large ship, now moving slowly and cautiously upriver, arrived at the docks at Wilmington, and when the hull bumped against the rough wooden wharf, a loud, happy cry arose from the passengers after more than nine weeks confined to the ship.

Margaret ran up to Will and took his hand. "Isn't it marvelous!" she cried. "We're here! We're actually in America!"

He turned to her, almost wishing they hadn't yet reached the end of their voyage. "Aye, Margaret. But your journey isn't over yet. Your Da told me you'll soon board smaller vessels and go on further into the back country." He knew he would miss Margaret as she and her family moved on, and he stayed in Wilmington.

Her enthusiasm dampened. "Aye. He's determined to reach a place called Cross Creek, where a lot of Argyll Scots have already settled. I've overheard him and Mam talking about it. I think it was the only reason Mam agreed to make this journey, since there were others of our land already there. Pa is hoping to secure some land and make a new life for us there."

Will was called to help tie the ship to the dock and proceed with offloading the passengers, not one of which seemed the least bit eager to stay aboard, despite the late hour. He heard the bosun's whistle commanding attention and saw Captain Taylor standing on the wharf next to another man who was dressed as a fine gentleman.

"Ladies and gentlemen," the captain shouted. "Here to welcome us safely to the shores of North Carolina is its esteemed Royal Governor, Gabriel Johnston."

The travelers, obviously unsure about how to respond to this, gave light applause. Will could tell all they wanted at the moment was to disembark and plant their feet on the ground again. But Governor Johnston smiled and raised his hand in welcome.

"Fellow Scotsmen," he said, "we are happy to welcome you to this new land of opportunity."

Scotsman? Will was surprised. He had expected only Englishmen in positions of power on this shore. Johnston continued a short welcoming speech, after which Captain Taylor informed the immigrants that lodgings were available in Wilmington for those who wished to seek them out. Or, he invited, they could stay on board the *Orion* if they so wished.

A few took him up on that offer, having no money for lodging, but the majority made their way off the ship and onto dry land. "I'll sleep under the stars if I have to," Will heard one man say as he stepped onto the wharf. "No more ocean for me!"

When all were on shore who wanted to go ashore and the ship was secured, crew members gleefully left for the nearest pubs. "Come along, Will," Simpson invited, much to Will's surprise and delight. "You've been one of us, and I must say, for a...young man...you've given great service. I'd like t' buy you a pint."

Honored as he was to be included, Will wanted to say goodbye to Margaret and Mr. McKinney, even to Esther and Mary, whom he'd come to know better on the voyage. But looking around, he saw they must have already left in search of lodgings for the night. They would be back on the morrow, he reckoned, to claim and carry away their belongings. His goodbyes could be said then.

He turned to Mr. Simpson. "I thank you kindly, sir, and accept."

The late June night was warm as they made their way through the streets of Wilmington toward a pub, and Will's heart was pounding with both excitement and trepidation. Captain Taylor had joined them, and as Mr. Simpson pushed through the doorway of the steamy bar, Will saw that many of the crew were already assembled, drinks in hand.

Among the throng he also saw a number of the men who had been passengers on the voyage, including Mr. McKinney, who raised his glass when he saw them come in. "Gents," he called out in his hearty voice. "Here's t' th' health of the most seaworthy vessel, *Orion*," he toasted, "and to its intrepid captain and crew. May they always have fair winds and following seas." Cheers went up, and Will joined in heartily. And then he saw McKinney raise his glass and his gaze specifically toward him, and he realized with no small measure of both astonishment and gratification that McKinney was acknowledging that Will, too, had been part of that intrepid crew.

***

The following morning Will hauled lines and off-loaded the many heavy trunks, crates, and parcels that had been stowed both in steerage and in the hold. Passengers, united by the trials of the ocean voyage, mingled on the dock and in a nearby park saying their farewells. Some were headed to the back country, others remaining in town. Will caught sight of Margaret running toward him, her bonnet flying off her blond curls.

"Will, what will you do now?" she asked him again.

He brushed his hands free of the grime of the heavy ropes. "Don't exactly know," he replied, giving her the same answer as earlier. "Was thinking of looking around here to see if there's a smithy in town that needs a hand."

Behind Margaret, Fergus McKinney approached. "Well, Will, I ken you've got plans from here?"

Will dropped his head and studied his rough boots. "No, sir, can't say as I have anything definite. Something'll show itself, I'm certain." He gave a rueful laugh. "One thing I'm also certain of, I'm not cut out for the life of a sailor, although Captain Taylor has offered to retain me."

"Why not come with us?" McKinney invited. "We're headed to the back country, and Esther and me and the girls, well, we talked about it last night. We could use your help. Strong young man like you would be of great service to us as we get ourselves acquainted with this new land. And," he added with a grin, "if you're with us, we can count you in our headright when we go to apply for a land grant. The more heads, the more land."

Will wasn't sure what he was talking about, but it sounded like a good offer, better than any other option he had. Margaret had mentioned this before while they were still on the ship, and Will had shrugged it off, but now the offer was made by Mr. McKinney himself. Fergus McKinney was different from his own Da in some ways, but much like him in others. It took Will less than five seconds to say yes. "I would be greatly honored, sir, and I will work hard for you."

In spite of this offer, he was apprehensive, recalling the captain's description of America as a wild, unsettled land, but he'd overheard McKinney and some of the others speak of the new settlement at Cross Creek, how it was safe from the Indians who'd been run off in earlier wars. Will knew nothing about Indians, other than they were apparently savage and vicious, and he had no wish to encounter them.

The newcomers rested in Wilmington for a fortnight before undertaking this second leg of their journey. Will accompanied McKinney to a land office, where Fergus handled some business and was given papers that would enable him to file for a land grant once they arrived in the back country and found the land they wished to settle. It all seemed too easy to Will. No one owned land in the Highlands except the clan chiefs and the lairds. He knew McKinney had been a tacksman for a laird, a position of power and some wealth, but even that did not entitle him to own land. Now, just barely off the boat, he was being given the right to own his own property.

Will was nothing short of astounded, and sadly wished his own Da had been able to come to this wonderful new world.

The men in the group assembled at the docks the morning they were scheduled to leave to help load their goods and supplies onto lighters, longboats, and even canoes for the arduous trip upriver. A few backed out on going further, stating they had no taste for getting into another boat, but McKinney reminded them of who'd paid for their passage to their ultimate destination and asked to be partially reimbursed if they chose to stay in Wilmington. Only one family did so.

Among the laborers who had been hired to help load and guide the flotilla were a number of people with black skins. They looked strange and exotic to Will, but they spoke his native Gaelic as they worked with the Highlanders. At mid-morning, the women and children arrived at the dock, ready to embark. One of the women apparently overheard a black-skinned man speaking to Mr. McKinney in Gaelic and fell to the ground in a near-faint. Her husband ran to her. "Felicity! What is it? What is wrong?"

The woman, fanning herself with one hand, pointed to the black man. "Is...is this what's t' happen t' us, Alexander? 'Tis it so hot here our skin will turn black?"

Mr. McKinney helped Alexander bring his wife back to her feet, then said, "No, those people are from Africa, Felicity. They're born black. They've come to this country from afar, same as we."

Will found the whole business curious; there was something not being said about how and why black Africans came to America and spoke the tongue of the Highlanders, but he asked no questions.

At last, the voyagers and their belongings were on board the various vessels, and Will helped push the boat carrying the McKinneys and one other family away from the dock and into the river. The current flowed against them, but he joined the others who manned the paddles, and slowly they began to make headway. The river was wide at Wilmington, and as they moved upstream, it narrowed but remained navigable. At places, it had cut high bluffs to one side. Will saw that much of the land had already been settled, with plantation houses set back from the river and crops thriving in the rich soil between.

They camped along the river several nights, and Fergus McKinney boosted their sometimes-drooping spirits with his fiddle music. Margaret was always good for a dance, and as she had on the ship, she often got Will to join in. After one particular long and exhausting dance, Will backed away and found a fallen tree to rest on and catch his breath. Margaret followed him, and he was gratified to see she was out of breath as well.

"Where'd your father learn to play the fiddle like that?" he asked.

Margaret laughed. "I don't know. He's played it my whole life. I think maybe his own Da taught him."

Will considered that a moment. "I'd like to learn to play it someday," he mused, thinking it would be better to play the music than dance to it.

* * *

Cross Creek was a small settlement with but a few dwellings surrounding a larger structure in the center. As Will and the others who rowed the boats nestled them into the muddy embankment, he saw a small crowd of people running toward them, smiling and waving, welcoming them in Gaelic. Their enthusiastic greeting warmed Will's heart, and he realized suddenly how worried he had been over what they would find when they finally arrived at this place.

A tall, fair-haired man broke through the gathering. "Ah, 'tis you at last, Fergus McKinney?"

McKinney stepped from the canoe into the shallow water and waded up to the shore. "Aye. Do you be Duncan Campbell?"

"Aye." And the two embraced as if they were long lost brothers.

Will turned to Margaret. "Do you know him?"

"No, but he is the man Da has corresponded with for many months, organizing this voyage and making sure we had a safe destination. I think," she added, "he's the land agent's representative, the one we're to get our land from."

After the boats were unloaded and the goods were safely stashed inside the large central building, the women brought food—roasted corn, an orange potato-looking thing, venison, blackberries, and freshly baked bread. After the meager fare on the ship and bare necessities for the trip upriver, Will's mouth watered at the fragrance. But Duncan Campbell raised his hand and called for silence.

"Let us pray," he said. And then he proceeded to offer thanks for the safe arrival of the newcomers, asked for protection and continued good harvests, and then blessed the food. "Amen."

Will was seated next to Margaret and Mary at a long table with the rest, and he tucked into this veritable feast with shameless enthusiasm. He hadn't realized how hungry and tired he was, and he saw the others devouring the meal with equal zeal.

Some of the citizens of Cross Creek offered to take in a few of the newcomers, who seemed in some way kin to them. The rest were to sleep in the central meeting house, which Will learned served many purposes, including a church. These people were devout Presbyterians, the same as his parents, and he was comforted by that familiarity. He knew Catholicism had been behind the conflict over the Jacobean cause, but his family had long ago left that faith and converted to the Calvinist teachings. But truth be told, he had no strong religious convictions either way. In fact, he wished only to be left alone in that regard. In spite of what Simpson had told him about the struggle for the throne of England, it was religion, he believed, that had killed his father, his clansmen, and his way of life. He had no real use for it anymore.

CHAPTER SIX

Cross Creek, North Carolina, August 1749

On a hot night in August, three years later, Will was bunked down in his small space in the smithy he and Fergus had built on their farm shortly after they arrived in Cross Creek. The McKinney family lived close by in their own cabin. He was awakened to the sound of Fergus McKinney's fiddle and giggles from the two girls who had become like sisters to him in the years he had known them. Well, almost like sisters. As he had grown from boy to man, his feelings for Margaret had changed in unexpected and unfamiliar ways.

"Wake up, Will!" Fergus's voice boomed through the doorway.

Will slid out of bed and hastily donned his breeches. "Coming, sir!" What had happened? What was going on? He opened the rough wooden door and peered out to find the family assembled in front of him. "What...?"

But before he could finish his question, Fergus struck up a fiddle tune he recognized as a celebration song, and Margaret, Mary, and even Esther, shouted, "Happy birthday!"

Will's birthday had never been celebrated before, not at home and not in the new land. He'd never really known the actual date. "What?" he exclaimed again with a bemused smile.

"Come along inside the house, son. We've a hearty breakfast waiting for ye."

Will followed them into the cozy cabin, and Esther offered him a steaming cup of coffee. Then Fergus plunked the fiddle strings and announced, "'Tis your sixteenth birthday, Will, and we've a present for you." He handed the fiddle to Will. "You've been learning to play, and you have a right fair hand at it now."

Will looked at the fiddle and saw it wasn't the battered instrument Fergus played, but a different one. It looked new. "What? Where did you get this?"

"I had Mr. Smythe at the mercantile find one for me. I'm glad it arrived in time."

Will struggled with his emotions. Fergus McKinney was the kindest man, whose generosity never ceased to amaze him. He looked up at Fergus, then at Esther and the two girls. "Thank you," he said simply, then placed it under his chin and played a short riff. "I'm not as good as you," he said to Fergus, "but I'll keep trying."

But Fergus wasn't through with him. "Sixteen's a major passing date for a young man, Will. Time to sign you up for the militia, same as me."

Will had no wish to take up arms again, but he knew it was the law in the colony. "Aye," was all he said.

"But first," Fergus continued, "we have a trial for you, to test your readiness for manhood. The *clach cuid fir*, the lifting stone."

Will tried to think of when he'd last heard of this ritual. He'd been young and had paid it little mind when his cousins were subjected to it, other than to hope he never had to perform it. "I, uh, didn't know it was my birthday. Are you sure of it?"

Fergus laughed. "You told me it was in late summer, and I had to give a date for you to get the headright for the land, you see, so today's the date I wrote down on the paperwork. So it's officially yours, whether it be actual or not."

Will loved Fergus McKinney as if he were his own father. The man had taken him under his wing and treated him like a son, and there was no way he was going to argue about this. "So, what's with this *clach cuid fir*, sir?" To Will's mind, with all the timber he'd felled and lifted and the iron he'd forged into heavy utensils in the smithy, surely he'd passed this test long ago.

Fergus opened the front door of the cabin, which had been built of pine from the trees they had taken down to clear the land. To Will's horror, a small group of people he recognized as neighbors from nearby farms had quietly gathered while he was eating breakfast. When they saw him, they set up a huzzah, and then parted to show him a large stone that sat on the ground nearby.

"Where'd that come from?" he asked Fergus quietly. As far as Will knew, he'd cleared every stone he'd encountered in preparing the land for cultivation.

Fergus gave out his hearty laugh. "Why, they brought it just for you, Will, to celebrate this important birthday."

Will had to laugh a little as well. "And now I'm t' pick it up, or not be called a man?"

"Something like that."

Will strode to the stone. It looked like he might be able to lift it, but it was larger than most he'd cleared away. He hesitated, until he heard a female voice say, "Go on, Will. You can do it."

Margaret. Will's face flushed. There was no question of *if*. He *must* do it. He could not stand to humiliate himself in front of her. And besides, he wanted to be proven a man, and possibly, he'd been thinking of late, worthy of her hand when she grew older. Fergus had organized this trial. He must not fail.

Without glancing in Margaret's direction, he squatted in front of the stone. He felt of its smooth surface and measured its size with his arms. He inhaled deeply and said a silent invocation to whatever powers held sway over mortal men, then finding his hold, slowly lifted the huge boulder until it reached his waist, which he knew to be the requisite height for the test.

Around him, his friends and neighbors cheered, and he saw Margaret out of the corner of his eye, doing a little dance of glee. For a moment, he forgot himself, and the big rock slipped from his hands, landing squarely on his right foot before rolling away. The pain was instant and overpowering, and he had to bite his lips to keep from crying out. He bent over in agony and looked at the damage. Being rousted from sleep and abruptly called forward, he had not donned his boots, and his bare toes paid the price. His toes and part of his upper foot were torn and bleeding, but it was his big toe that alarmed him. It was now sitting at an odd angle, pointing away from the rest of the toes.

Margaret, now fourteen and self-assured as she, too, passed from childhood to adult, ran to him. "Oh, Will, oh, no!"

Esther was on Margaret's heels. "Such nonsense," she muttered, glaring at Fergus. "Now look at what you've gone and done."

Before he could protest, Margaret and Esther hauled Will bodily back inside the cabin and dropped him roughly onto one of the chairs he'd built. His big toe burned like fire.

A woman from the village followed them inside. "Let me set it if it's broken," she said without asking permission. "I've set bones more times than I'd like to know."

Will looked up and saw others had followed her into the cabin. "I...I'll be all right," he managed, but he wasn't at all sure that was the truth. However, now that he was truly a man, initiated by rite and all that, he couldn't show any weakness.

"Bosh," the woman said. She turned to Fergus and barked. "Get me a small but strong and straight piece of wood." To Esther, she said, "Have you clean rags about? And some whisky?"

Will knew very well there was whisky on the premises, but he'd promised Fergus not to mention it to his wife and daughters. They'd built a small still that they kept hidden in the nearby woods, and from the corn harvest each year they brewed a few batches which Fergus sold to earn extra money. Esther didn't approve of spirits, so her husband was careful to keep this activity hidden, and Will wasn't about to betray him now. He wasn't sure what the woman needed whisky for anyhow.

But Margaret suddenly dashed to the door. "I'll get it." Esther stared after her in surprise, but then hurried to find some rags from fabric she'd woven for their household.

When Fergus returned with the splint, he was with Margaret, who held a clay jar in the crook of one arm and her chin high. Fergus's face was crimson, but he said nothing, just handed the healing woman the wooden splint. Margaret passed her the whisky jug. Esther produced the rags, which the woman tore into strips to bind the splint to his toe. She sat on a chair next to Will's, raised his foot to her lap, surveyed the injured toe, then asked for a cup, into which she poured not a small amount of whisky. "Here," she said, handing it to Will. "Drink it. You'll need it for the pain."

Will had partaken of the whisky before and not found it much to his liking. He looked over at Fergus, who only nodded grimly. "Go on, do as she says, son."

Will sipped the burning liquid and couldn't suppress a shudder as it went down. He coughed over the raggedness in his throat. Then the woman suddenly grabbed his toe and gave it a yank that almost sent him into blindness with pain. The next moment, she gave it a shove to straighten it back in its proper place, poured some of the whisky on it, and began to tie the splint to it with the rag strips. Will had to work hard not to throw up. As if she read his mind, the woman instructed Margaret to give him another shot of whisky.

"There," she said at last, taking a long look at her work. "It pains you now, but in time, it'll be good as new," she assured him, pouring a bit of whisky over her own hands and wiping them on remnants of the rags.

Fergus had ushered the curious onlookers out of the cabin, and he thanked the healer, offering to pay her for helping. She refused money but allowed as how she'd appreciate a wee dram of the whisky to take home.

When everyone had left, Esther turned her full glare onto Fergus. "Whisky! You've been makin' whisky?"

Fergus returned her glare. "Aye, wife. And I will continue. I don't drink it, well, at least not much. I sell it."

"Sell it!" Esther almost shouted at him. "Sell it? The devil's own drink!"

Fergus's expression softened. He went to her and put his big arms around her small shoulders. "Aye, wife. I sell it. How do you think we can afford to buy iron for the smithy, or that new milk cow we just got?"

Esther sobbed, then turned and ran into the small room at the other end of the house that was their quarters. Margaret and Mary looked on in wide-eyed astonishment. Will just wanted to disappear.

"I'm sorry, Mr. McKinney. I didn't mean to drop the stone." What a silly thing to say, he thought, but he didn't know what else to say to fill the awkward silence.

McKinney looked at the three of them, and then suddenly burst into laughter. "Of course you didn't, son. No man in his right mind would do that on purpose. And now the cat is out of the bag on the whisky, which is good."

Will looked at him in surprise, feeling a warm glow from the whisky beginning to numb his senses just a bit. "Good?" He didn't think Esther found it so good.

"Aye. I've been feeling bad about keeping that secret. Esther and I have never kept secrets. It's just as well she found out."

"Da," Margaret interjected. "Sorry, but I think Mam knew. She just pretended to be surprised. I found her once in the smithy poking around, and I think she found your jugs. She didn't want to believe it, so she looked the other way."

"Ho, ho!" Fergus laughed harder. "So, more secrets are outed today. Hey, Will, have you any secrets you want to share?"

But Will wanted only one thing—for the pain to go away. "Nay, sir, other than that before this moment, I didn't care for the taste of whisky, but right now, I'd give a lot for another dash."

Will's toe healed, but it was never straight again, mainly because he grew tired of the impediment of the splint and after a couple of days, he took it off. With it on, he wasn't able to wear his boot on that foot and working in the field with one bare foot wasn't comfortable. His toe still hurt when he put his boot on again at last, but, as he pointed out to Margaret, the confinement of the leather held his toe in place, at least to some degree.

Will found himself seeking every opportunity to be with Margaret. If she needed to go to market, he drove the wagon. If she needed help with the laundry, he was there. Sometimes he caught himself just gazing at her, watching her flower into a beautiful young woman. Soon he would ask for her hand.

Chapter Seven

Cross Creek, South Carolina, September 1752

The community of Cross Creek continued to grow as more immigrants arrived. Some were Highlanders like themselves, but there were many others from the Lowlands, Ireland, even Germany. Slowly the daily use of Gaelic gave way to English, mainly by necessity. With so many different languages and dialects mingled together, it was simpler to adopt the language of the English colony. Cross Creek, small as it was, had become a center of commerce between the Piedmont of North Carolina and the Cape Fear River, although most major trading remained with Charlestown in South Carolina. Most of the traders were English speakers as well, so it became the language of commerce, and Will, Margaret, and Mary spoke, read, and wrote in English.

The people of Cross Creek, to Will's amazement considering many were Highland Scots, were supportive of the English king, something he swore he could never be. It was the king's own son, Cumberland, or the soldiers under his command, who had killed his father and friends. His dream of Duncan's death was coming with less frequency, but still it stalked him at times. He would never forgive the English. But many of his friends followed the lead of Duncan Campbell, the land surveyor who was loyal to the English king down to his toes.

Will found it awkward when he was with them in town, and the talk turned to politics. They never asked him directly about his own loyalty, probably because he mostly left their company before the issue arose. It was clear to him that unlike himself, they had come for the land, not for freedom from English domination.

One day, upon his return to the farm from taking some of their produce to Cross Creek for sale, Fergus returned to the cabin, clearly agitated. Will was on the front porch, sharpening farm tools and figured the older man was cross having been caught in a gale that came upon them unexpectedly from the direction of the ocean. Rain had come down in a slanted deluge, whipped by strong winds, and Fergus was drenched. He barely grunted a greeting before he went inside. Will paid little attention to him until he caught the drift of sharp conversation from inside. He respected the privacy of husband and wife, but he didn't leave his seat, curious to hear what was going on.

"Get me a dry shirt, would you please, wife?" Fergus said politely, but his voice was almost a growl, so unlike him. "And some hot coffee."

Will heard her bustle about, and then the sound of a tin mug slamming down onto the table. "Damn!" Fergus muttered.

"Fergus, don't swear," Esther scolded, then said, "What is it? What is the matter? Has something happened in Cross Creek?"

"No," he replied at first, then, "Well, yes." A long pause, then, "I'm torn."

"Torn? Between what?"

Will was all ears now. Rarely had he seen Fergus McKinney in such a state. "While I was in the village, Campbell approached me, said some newcomers wanted to buy land. Most of the land around here is already taken, so there's no land grants available nearby."

Esther didn't reply, and Will held his breath. Eventually Fergus went on. "Campbell told me what was being offered for acreage such as ours, good land already cleared and not so far from the river." He paused, then said, "Esther, I didn't come here to make a fortune, but this sorely tempts me. We got this land for free, and now we can make a pretty penny by selling it and moving on."

Will heard a pan crash to the floor. "What?" Esther exclaimed. "Are you mad?"

Fergus gave a low laugh. "Probably. But hear me out. We left Scotland on a chance that this would bring us a better life, and it has, as hard as it has been at times. We've built this farm into something that is worth good money, if we choose to take it. If we move on, we will go with money in our pockets, a goodly sum, I might add."

"But...but won't we just have to turn around and spend that money to start over again? I don't see where there's a gain."

"I spoke of that to Campbell, and he's told me there's good land up in the Piedmont, in the Granville District," he said. "Fertile land to be had for the asking, with just a small fee to register the grant. And," he added, "I hear you can see mountains from there. Can't go into the mountains, he says, because it's Indian land. But losh! What I would give to see mountains again! This hot, flat place has burned a bit of my soul."

Will was astounded but at the same time, elated. He, too, had sorely missed the mountains of his homeland, and like McKinney, he disliked the heat and humidity of Cross Creek. But it was difficult to think of giving up all they'd worked for and the friends they'd made.

That evening after supper, Fergus broached the subject to his family, including Will. He repeated what Will had overheard, adding that instead of holding only one hundred acres as they did now, they would be eligible to claim one square mile, six hundred and forty acres along the Yadkin River. "I hear it's the most beautiful region, abounding in game, plentiful fish in the river."

"We have that here," Esther said flatly. "Are there wolves?"

"Yes, wife, but we have those here too."

"What about Indians, Da?" Margaret asked.

"Like I said, Campbell told me that the Indian land is west of there, across the Blue Ridge mountains. They'll likely not bother us in the Piedmont."

"Not likely!" Mary cried out. "Are you not sure about that, Da?"

"Well, others have gone there before us," he hedged. "I've not heard of any complaints."

Will spoke up at last. "When will we...I mean, would we move on, sir?"

Fergus's eyes lit up. "As soon as we can make arrangements, if you are all in agreement, that is. This move will be different, as we have more to move. Will has built furniture, and there's Esther's spinning wheel and loom that must go with us. We will want to take the smithy equipment and supplies, and our farm tools, the cow, maybe hogs for breeding, and chickens. We will need to buy at least two horses to help us along our way."

Will could see the eagerness building in his friend and mentor, and apparently it was catching, because Margaret jumped up and said, "I think we should do it, Da!" Then she looked furtively at Will as if to make sure he agreed with her. He grinned and shrugged. It wasn't his decision to make, but he thought it worth considering.

Esther remained silent, and Mary started to cry. But in the end, the family agreed among them that making a move further inland for more land and the profit to be made from selling their land in Cross Creek was the most advantageous decision for their future.

Fergus and Will conferred later as to the best time to make the move. Fergus was anxious to go now that the decision had been made, but Will pointed out it was September and there were still crops to be harvested. "It might be wiser to wait until spring, sir," he suggested. "It's further north, and I believe winters will be colder there. We wouldn't have any shelter against that until we build again."

Fergus looked at him with what Will perceived to be in a new light. "Well thought out," he said. "I suppose there will still be buyers for this land in the spring."

Will drew in a deep breath, summoning courage. Now seemed to be a good time to talk with Fergus about something that had been on his mind a lot lately. "There is one thing, sir, I need to speak with you about."

'Yes?"

"It's...it's about Margaret, sir. She's of marriageable age now, and I as well. I...uh, well, we wish to wed, sir." There! He'd said it!

Will wasn't certain what he was expecting, but it wasn't McKinney's bold laughter. "Well, son, I was wondering if you was ever going to get around to that. Do you think I've not missed the way the two of you have mooney eyes for each other? And I saw you steal a kiss the other day out in the smithy."

Will's cheeks burned. "I'm sorry, sir. I've tried hard to be respectful of her, and of your family. You've treated me like a son, and well, I wasn't sure if that made my feelings for Margaret inappropriate. But she's not my kin sister," he added quickly.

"Aye. That she is not. And you've long been the son I had always wanted, if not by blood, then by merit. Now you will truly be my son. You have my blessing."

Will let out his breath. His hands were clammy, and he'd broken out into a sweat as if he'd been plowing the field. "I thank you, sir."

"Does Esther know of this?"

"Nay, unless Margaret has spoken to her. We wanted to ask you first. If you forbade us, we said we'd honor your decision." Then Will broke into a wide grin. "Thank you again, sir. May I go and tell Margaret the good news?"

"Aye. But we must then tell Esther and Mary. I'm sure they won't be very surprised."

* * *

Will and Margaret were married in a ceremony at the central meeting house when an itinerant Presbyterian preacher, arranged for by Duncan Campbell, arrived in Cross Creek. Their vows were taken in English, because the preacher spoke no Gaelic, but Will and Margaret had decided beforehand to repeat each vow in Gaelic as well, because some of the older members of the community had never learned English.

Will was slightly embarrassed that night when Margaret left the room she'd shared with Mary and moved into Will's meager quarters in the smithy, but there was no other place for them to spend their first night together. Fergus had promised to build them a cabin on their new land as a wedding gift, and Will would be glad when they had a place of their own.

Months later, with the harvest in, jugs of corn whisky made and sold, and stores laid in that might be harder to come by in their new home, the family prepared to move on. The winter solstice was behind them, and a begrudging Esther was somewhat ameliorated by a promise of a larger house to be built for her and a second for Margaret. In early March, the McKinneys sold their property for more than Fergus had expected, and they left Cross Creek accompanied by two other families who had made the same decision. On a cold, rainy day, the small caravan headed north on the trading path into the next "new world."

CHAPTER EIGHT

Yadkin River Valley, North Carolina, Spring 1753

"It's beautiful!" Margaret exclaimed as they topped a rise and viewed an expansive valley along the Yadkin River. It was late afternoon, and the sun's rays struck the new grasses, turning them golden. Budding leaves on huge sycamore and tulip trees shimmered a pale yellow-green, and a few flowering trees peeked out from the woodlands as if in welcome. Will had to swallow over the hardness in his throat. This was a far more inviting land than either the north of Scotland or the scorching sandy hills of Cross Creek. He was glad they'd made this decision, as difficult as this journey had been.

The families from Cross Creek who'd undertaken this new adventure together, the McKinneys, the newly married Gordons, the Patersons, and the Murreys, had trudged through mud and rain for a good part of the trip, sleeping beneath their wagons and building a fire when they could find dry wood. They'd met others on the way, some taking the weather challenges in good humor, others soured by the gray skies and constant wind.

At last, they'd reached their first destination, a small settlement just north of the Granville Line referred to as Salisbury although it had no official name. There, the men in their party met with the land agent for John Carteret, Lord Granville, who was in England but who owned this land clear to the far western oceans, or so they were told, but who was eager to populate his North Carolina holdings to increase their value.

"Well, Lord Granville is in luck," Fergus said with his usual good humor. "We're here to do just that. Tell me, sir, what land is it that we might claim for a grant?"

The agent frowned. "I need to make clear the terms upon which Lord Granville will allow settlement," he said. "First, it's not an outright grant. It's a patent for which you must apply. If you are accepted there will be a fee of five pounds to register your claim, the cost of a survey, and after the land is turned over to you, there will be a quitrent of five shillings each year."

Will glanced over at Fergus and saw that the equanimity had left his expression. "That is not what we were told, sir. We came here under the impression that we could obtain a grant to up to six hundred and forty acres free of any costs or future rents save a small application fee."

"Then your impression was wrong," the agent answered sharply. "Whoever told you that didn't know the facts, obviously."

It had been Duncan Campbell who'd told that to Fergus, Will was certain, and his mind grew suspicious. Had Campbell somehow made money from orchestrating the sale of their farm to the newcomers? It would be like him, he who licked the English boots.

Fergus, with Will by his side, acted unperturbed. "Well, sir, we are here now, and we intend to find good land to settle and farm. Do you have ideas of where we might find such land?"

The agent studied the four men for a long moment, then replied, "The richest land lies to the northwest, along the Yadkin River. It's the edge of the frontier in North Carolina, but not yet claimed. It's past the Wachovia Tract by about twenty miles."

"What's the Wachovia Tract?" Will wanted to know.

"Bunch of Germans have bought near a hundred thousand acres from Lord Granville," he said, looking at the map that lay on the table between them. "Call themselves Moravians, but they're German speaking. This fall, they plan to start building there, but they've got bigger plans than that. Here," he said, pointing to a place on the map, "is the western border of their tract. So any place to the west of this line is open for settlement at present." He paused, then added, "I wouldn't go too far west, however. The Indians don't live there, but they roam and hunt those woods, and, well, they don't much like white folks."

Will considered this as the agent continued to outline what it would take for them to lay claim to the land. "First, select the land you wish to acquire, set out and register a claim with this office, which will then petition Lord Granville for a patent on your behalf." It seemed to Will far more complicated than their acquisition had been in Cross Creek, this one having to do with surveys and permissions. And, unlike they'd been led to believe, quitrents.

As they left the tent that served as a makeshift home for the legal needs of the new community, Will remarked, "I thought this was to be free land, sir, or for only a small fee."

"Fergus. Call me Fergus if you won't call me Da."

Though he loved Fergus, Will found it difficult to call him what he'd called his own father. "Fergus, then. Will we be paying rent to the Earl, just like back in Scotland?"

"That's what I understand now, although I did not think that the case when we left Cross Creek."

Will could tell he was disgruntled. He waited a while, then asked, "Are you sorry we came?"

Fergus sighed and stretched his long arms out in the direction of their next destination. "Why be sorry? We're here, and we'll make it work. Besides," he added with a wry grin, "I bet it sometimes takes years to get all that fancy paperwork together."

The families decided to remain together and settle as neighbors, believing it would be safer out there on the edge of the wilderness. The Patersons were a milling family from the Lowlands of Scotland, and the Murreys were farmers from Ulster. In this new land of America, it seemed to Will not to matter so much where you came from as it did where you were going. Fergus was right. We're here, all of us, and we'll make it work.

Within a week, they had reached this valley, and to a person they agreed it was worth the difficult journey. "'Tis beautiful indeed," Will said as his eyes scanned the horizon. "But I see no mountains."

He and Fergus stood up on the seat of the wagon, hoping for a glimpse of the blue ridges they'd been promised, but all that met their eyes was a wild, untamed stretch of deciduous and pine trees. "We could move on west," Will suggested, but Fergus shook his head.

"I can't ask Esther and the girls to move out there," he said in a low voice. "You heard what that man said about the Indians. This land is flat enough that we can cultivate good fields, the river is nearby for Paterson to build his mill, and maybe in time, we can venture into the mountains, even if it's just for a hunt. I don't want to push on further, Will."

The families made camp on the rise above the valley, and over the next few days, the men rode along the river and through the woods, looking at the lay of the land and at last arriving at agreement as to who was going to claim which parcel. Their arrangement was sealed by handshakes, but Will chose to describe each section in writing and illustrated the document with a rough sketch. "We'll need these markers for the surveyors," he said to the others, "so we might as well define them now." The markers comprised landmarks such as large rocks, a bend in the river, and numerous old tree trunks.

The McKinney and Gordon lands abutted the river at a large curve, with the Paterson section to the north and the Murrey holdings to the south, all of them along the eastern banks of the Yadkin. Will, Margaret, and the McKinneys set up temporary quarters beneath a canvas sheet stretched over a large tree branch and tied to other branches. The canopy provided shelter from sun and rain, but wind easily breezed beneath and above it, testing the strength of both rope and the branches that secured it.

Will and Fergus began clearing their new property, felling trees that would soon be turned into their cabins. The five of them walked the land and selected the sites for their new homes, and the men started setting the rocks in place for the foundations. Between the two structures, Esther and Mary began tilling the soil for a kitchen garden, while Margaret worked on laying a wooden fence that would enclose the milk cow and hogs. The chickens roamed free until some were discovered missing, prey to the wild creatures nearby, after which at night they were put back in the crates they had traveled in.

"We must get our seeds in the ground as soon as possible," Esther told them over supper one evening as they sat together on logs around the campfire. "It's nearly summer."

Indeed, the air was warm and fragrant with the scent of newly turned earth. Tiny creatures peeped and croaked from the wetlands, and the days were slowly growing longer. Will lounged against the log, holding Margaret's hand and thinking how lucky he was. The land was lush and giving, he had a beautiful wife, and Margaret had just whispered to him that there would be a baby come winter.

Suddenly Mary gave out a blood-curdling scream and pointed at something across the river. Will jumped up and reflexively reached for his long rifle, which they'd been advised to always keep close at hand. In the twilight he spotted four figures on horseback across the river. From their dress, Will knew who had come to call.

"Indians," he said. "Stay here," he told the women, and he and Fergus, guns at the ready, moved cautiously across the newly cleared land and into the cover of the large trees that grew at the river's edge.

On the far side of the river, one of the Indians held up his hand and called out in English. "Food. We are hungry."

"Catawbas," Will guessed in a low voice. He hadn't seen many Indians, but there'd been a few in the Salisbury settlement when they'd arrived. These were clothed in similar manner, in buckskin and leggings, but they had painted circles around their eyes, one white, one black. The hair rose on the back of Will's neck until Fergus spoke.

"They're peaceful," he said. "Hungry. All they want is food. They're probably on their way south to their own villages."

Will had shot a deer that day, and the meat was cooking in the large iron pot Esther had suspended over the fire. "What should we do?"

"Feed them," Fergus answered simply. "We need their friendship. These are their ancestral hunting grounds after all."

Will recalled the land agent's comment about Indians not much liking white people, but he figured Fergus was right. He held up his hand and motioned for the group to cross the river and come to their campfire. When they returned to the women, Esther and Mary were not to be seen. Margaret's face was ashen, but she didn't flinch when Will told her the Indians had come for food, and that they were going to share their meal with them.

When the Catawbas reached the outer edges of the fire light, they dismounted, and the leader spoke to Fergus. "You are friend. We come in peace." He turned his gaze to the sizzling pot. "Hungry. Traveled far today. No game."

Will quickly went to the pot. With a long iron fork, he retrieved the venison steak from the kettle and placed it on a pan nearby. He took out his hunting knife and carved the meat into four pieces. It was to have been their dinner, and he was ravenous, but he served the Indians instead. They knew little about the natives of the region, and although they'd heard the Catawba were mostly friendly to the whites, he'd also heard a few stories about Indians perpetrating terrible acts upon the unprotected settlements. Better to placate them and give them what they needed rather than turn them away. It's possible they wouldn't be so friendly after that, maybe even harm the family to get food.

He handed the pan to the leader who took the largest piece, then passed it to the others. They ate with their fingers and quickly consumed the meat. Esther had made hoe cakes from corn meal they'd purchased in the settlement, and Will brought them to the Indians.

When they had finished eating, the leader turned to Fergus. "Thank you." And to Will. "Thank you." And with that, they remounted and rode into the darkness.

Esther and Mary emerged from the woods behind the canvas shelter after they were gone. "You gave them our food?" Esther cried when she learned what had taken place.

"Aye, wife. Better to give it than have it taken from us. Besides, we have more."

Will had already unwrapped what remained of the deer and carved another hunk of meat to go into the pot. "Margaret, could you make us some more hoe cakes, please?" he asked his wife.

Only when things returned to some semblance of normalcy did his heartbeat settle down. Indians! These had been peaceful, but he knew there were others. Would they be friend or foe? Or both? He vowed to learn more about these people who were so foreign to his ken.

Chapter Nine

Spring rains were frequent, and the river rose to where it was no longer fordable where the Indians had crossed, but unless a storm was violent, the newly arrived families worked steadily to establish livable shelters and scratch out the beginnings of their farms. By summer's end, Will and Margaret occupied their new cabin which they'd chosen to set on a rise overlooking the river. They had created a barn for the livestock next to which they set up a smithy, and Will let it be known to the neighboring farmers that he could shoe a horse or hammer a tool if they needed his skills. The chickens now had a small coop, and the family enjoyed eggs and fresh milk, fish from the river, and game from the land.

The weather had turned dry after the wet spring, but in spite of near-drought conditions by summer, the corn managed to provide an adequate first crop. Clearing the fields had proven easier than in the sandy hills near Cross Creek. Many large stones lay loose in the soil, which they'd gathered and used as foundations for their cabins and to build their hearths and chimneys. Esther's garden, nourished with extra water hauled from the river, produced cabbage, okra, potatoes, beans, squash, and several herbs known for their medicinal qualities. They'd also started seeds that would be transplanted when sturdy enough to provide apples and peaches in the future orchard.

Neighbors, including the Patersons and the Murreys, and the Boones from the other side of the river, gathered on Sundays at different homes for worship and to share a meal, followed by music and even some dancing, although some frowned on that happening on the Lord's day. But Margaret couldn't keep her feet still when Fergus and Will plied their bows to the fiddle strings, and she danced although with more caution as her pregnancy was advancing.

One sunny September Sunday, a stranger passed their way. A trader named Hiram Greenlee drove into their midst and greeted them as if they were old friends. "Halloo! Haven't passed this way in a while. Thought I'd drop by t' see what all has happened in this here valley in the last months."

He looked around at the small group of families who'd come this day to the McKinney farm. "Looks t' me like a lot has happened," he laughed. "Last time I was through here, weren't no settlers anywheres nearby."

He dismounted without invitation, but Will and Fergus stepped up to welcome him. He was a scruffy fellow, dressed in buckskin breeches, high-topped boots made of a soft leather, and a dirty white hunting shirt covered with a rough cloak. A battered sweat-stained hat bespoke its hard use. In his wagon, he carried European goods that he was going to trade with the Indians further to the west, he told them—guns and ammunition, iron pots, calico, blankets, glass beads, and other items.

"I'll be back through here come spring," he told the group as he sipped the chickory coffee Esther had brewed. "If I'm lucky, the Cherokee will have a good hunting season this winter, and I'll carry their pelts and furs back down to old Charlestown."

Hiram Greenlee turned out to be something of a news courier as well. He knew the ways of the Indians, both the Cherokee and the Catawba. He knew too how unhappy the tribes were that folks like those gathered here were infringing on their native lands. "There's going to be troubles," he said. "Mark my word. But," he added, "it's something of their own fault. Theirs, and folks like me who bring them things they've never had before, things they want, like all those goods I got in the wagon. One of them pots is for my Cherokee wife," he added with a grin.

At this several of the women let out a low murmur, but Will only smiled. Greenlee looked as rough as any Indian might, and Will imagined it got lonely on the trading trails.

Greenlee continued, "They've let us white folk move steadily into their hunting grounds in exchange for things like these."

Will sensed he could learn a lot from this man, and he was suddenly eager to question him on the ways of the natives. "Will you stay the evening with us, Greenlee?" he invited with a glance at Margaret, who nodded. The McKinneys and the Gordons sat by the fire later that night. Greenlee had accepted their invitation to dinner, and afterwards, seemed congenial and willing to answer Will's many questions.

"You said there'll be Indian troubles," Will broached the subject carefully. He didn't want to upset the women, but they had moved to what Greenlee had called the back of beyond, with no protection against threats of all kinds, be it Indians, wolves, or weather, except their own wits. Will wanted to know what they might be facing.

"It's a complicated matter," Greenlee began, staring into the flames in the hearth. "This here's Catawba land. Over yonder, over the mountain ridges is Cherokee land. Except they both have hunted these hills and valleys for hundreds of years. Y'see, the Indians don't believe anybody owns the land. That their Great Spirit put them here, and the land is for their use, but they don't own it. That's one reason they've so easily allowed settlers to come into what has always been their territory. They figure the settlers don't own it either and that the Great Spirit meant for it to be shared by all of His creatures. But the whites don't see it that way."

Will thought about Lord Granville and his claim to a wide swath of North Carolina, and the land grants and quitrents he used to enrich himself. "But I heard there have been treaties that the English and Indians have agreed upon," he said.

Greenlee snorted. "Treaties made. Treaties broken. Them poor trusting Indians keep signing away what they think are the rights to live and work on the land, but not ownership. And the English keep breaking their promises not to move on further into what's supposed to be off limits."

"What are they like, the Indians?" Margaret asked.

Greenlee smiled. "They, too, are complicated, Mrs. Gordon. Most of them live peacefully in quiet villages, at least most of the time. The Catawbas live south of here, in South Carolina. The Cherokee have three clusters of villages, the Lower Towns down southwest, the Middle Towns in North Carolina, and the Overhill Towns over the Tanase."

"You said most of them live peacefully," Margaret said. "Does that mean we have nothing to fear?"

"I wish it were so," Greenlee sighed. "But I told you it was complicated. There are other tribes, you see, northern tribes that are ancient enemies of both the Cherokee and the Catawba. The Shawnee in particular. And for all the tribes, war has been a way of life forever. It is their way of attaining honor and status among themselves. Shawnee scalps are highly prized by the Cherokee, as are Cherokee and Catawba scalps to the Shawnee."

Will felt Margaret's hand slip into his. "How awful!" she uttered, unconsciously running the fingers of her other hand through her golden blond hair. Then her eyes widened, and she said, "Those Indians who came by here. Will said they came from the north. Were they Shawnee?"

Greenlee shrugged. "I doubt it. What did they look like?"

Will described their dress, and the painted circles around their eyes. "They were just hungry," he told the trader. "We gave them food, and they left us alone."

"Catawba. They paint their eyes like that when they go to war, so likely they were on their way back to their village somewhere south of here from fighting somewhere up north. Shawnee most likely." He spoke in a matter-of-fact way, indicating to Will this was nothing out of the ordinary. "But you were wise to give them what they needed. Like I said, they'll take it either way."

Fergus stood and stirred the fire. "What else do we need to know about the Indians?"

"Well, it's not just the Indians you need to know about. The French are stirring things up against the English, too."

Fergus grunted. "Never liked the French, but lots of Scots have French blood in their veins. What's happening that would affect us?"

"Again, it's about the land," Greenlee said. "The French claim a great deal of land all the way from Canada to the waters of the Gulf down New Orleans way. But there's some English settlers moving west out of Virginia and Pennsylvania into what the French consider their territory. The French are building forts all up and down to protect their interests. And," he added with a heaving sigh, "they're recruiting the Indians to help 'em. I wouldn't be surprised if they offered guns and trade goods in exchange for British scalps."

At this, Mary gave a little scream and covered her eyes, but Will got the picture in an instant. "So, the French might enlist the Cherokee, maybe even the Catawba, to fight the English should it come to war, and we would be at risk even though we mean no harm?"

Greenlee nodded. "Or it could go the other way. The Cherokee and Catawba have been good trading partners with the British. They don't wish to lose that status, or the trade goods." He chuckled. "Keeps me in business, you see."

"So, they would fight for the British, even though they're unhappy about us settlers taking their land and breaking treaties?" Margaret asked.

"If it's the best they can do. But if the French are able to offer them a better trade deal, they'll likely jump sides. You see, they aren't interested in the squabbles of the Europeans. They're interested in surviving these waves of strangers coming closer and closer and in holding onto their ancestral territories."

"Which they don't own," Esther blurted unexpectedly. "This is our land now, Mr. Greenlee. Or soon will be. We're applying for a patent from Lord Granville's agent, and..."

But she stopped when Greenlee held up a hand. "That is true, Mrs. McKinney, but only from the British point of view. To the Indians, this is still their territory, and they feel they have every right to whatever the land provides, including," he added grimly, "your crops. Maybe your livestock. Horses. I would take caution to protect yourselves and your farm, although if they decide to take something from you, they'll have it before you know it."

Mary started to sniffle. "I...I want to go home," she sobbed. "Or at least back to Cross Creek where we were safe."

Fergus stood and went to her, placing his large hands on her shoulders. "There now, no need to cry." Then he turned to Esther. "Maybe we best go back to our own cabin. Mary's upset by all this talk."

Esther rose and pulled her shawl over her shoulders. "As am I." She turned to Hiram Greenlee. "I bid you good night, sir. Your information is...interesting, but frightening. I wish to hear no more of it."

After they left, Will and Margaret sat with Greenlee late into the night, learning all they could about the complexity of the relationships between the French, the British, and the numerous Indian tribes, and even factions within those tribes. They found some consolation in learning that the Cherokee had peace chiefs as well as war chiefs. They were astounded that one named Attakulakula had actually traveled to England and met the king.

"He is a great diplomat," Greenlee told them. "But he faces young warriors, including his own son who is called Dragging Canoe, who are eager to make a name for themselves in battle." He shook his head. "I don't know what will come of this, but I advise you to buy arms and ammunition, and to teach the women how to use them too."

Greenlee declined their offer to sleep on the floor in front of the fireplace. "The wagon's my home and my bed when I'm on the road, and besides, if I'm sleeping on my goods, I know they're safe. I'll be off in the morning before daylight."

Before he left, he held out his hand to Margaret. "Thank you for your kind hospitality, Mrs. Gordon," he said, then glanced at her bulging belly. "Looks as if there'll be another Gordon sometime soon."

Will saw Margaret's face redden, but she smiled. "Aye, it's probably coming in January," she told him.

"There's no doctor out here," Greenlee pointed out, "but I know of a granny woman over th' mountain who might come if you need her."

"Granny woman?"

"Her name's Quella. Some call her a witch, others a wise woman. But all call on her when it's time for a birthin'. I'm headed her way. I could let her know there might be a need over on this side of th' mountain come January."

It hadn't occurred to Will that they might need a midwife to help Margaret along with her birthing, but Greenlee's words hit him like cold water. There were no doctors out here on the edge of nowhere. None of the family had medical training. What peril had he placed his wife in with this pregnancy? And worse, what would he ever do if he lost her?

"How far away does this woman live?"

"Two day's ride in good weather."

Will considered that. "But how would she know when to come? By the time we went to fetch her and bring her back, it would likely be too late."

Greenlee scratched his chin. "Well, if I let her know the babe's going to be here in January, she seems to have a way of knowin' when." He looked up at Will with a wry smile. "It's that part of her ways why folks call her a witch."

After Greenlee left, Will embraced Margaret, holding her tightly against him, wondering what kind of danger he'd placed her in. "Maybe we should have stayed in Cross Creek," he whispered into her soft hair.

She pulled away slightly and looked into his eyes. "No, Will. We have come here to make a new life, and we will be fine. I'm not afraid. Mam is here, and I've spoken to some of the women who come to our Sunday gatherings. There's a few who've born children in this new land who said they'd come help me. Besides," she added with a small laugh, "if you recall, I helped birth a calf right after we got here. It can't be that different."

CHAPTER TEN

January 1754

A full moon hung in the black night sky like a disc of ice, shining its cold reflection on the frost-covered fields as Will checked on the livestock in the barn. He shivered in spite of the woolen shirt and deerskin coat he wore. With no cloud cover, the night promised to be colder than any so far. He made his way across the light crust of frost to the cabin, his footsteps crunching in the icy glaze.

Inside, he found Margaret warming herself by the fire, one hand on her back, the other on her belly. "Are you all right?" he asked, closing the door securely against the cold and going to her.

She nodded slightly. "I am. But I think my time might be soon. I've been feeling strange pains in my back all afternoon." She clung to him. "Will," she said. "I...I sort of lied when I said I wasn't afraid of having this baby. That was before, and now it's time, I fear I might die in the birthing."

Will's heart dropped into the pit of his stomach. He didn't know how to reply. "Sit down," he said, leading her to the rocking chair he'd built for her. "I'll go fetch your mam," he said, heading swiftly out of the door again, overwhelmed suddenly with a sense of panic. Margaret was always the brave one. Fearless. Until now. And now, Will was filled with fear as well. Who and where were those women Margaret had said would come? How could he possibly bring them in time?

Esther and Mary had already gone to bed, and Fergus answered Will's pounding on the door. "What is it? What's happened?"

"It's Margaret. I...I think the baby's coming."

Fergus roused his wife and daughter, and in a few minutes, the four of them ran back to the Gordon's cabin. As he went up the steps, Will was alarmed to see the door slightly ajar. He was certain he'd secured it when he left.

When he opened it, he was astonished to see a strange woman sitting beside his wife on the bed, rubbing the back of Margaret's hand with her own long fingers, soothing her with a soft voice. Margaret looked up as nothing out of the ordinary had happened, her face serene. She appeared afraid no more. The woman turned to the family who stood aghast in the doorway.

"I've come to help the missus here with her birthing," she said simply, appearing unperturbed.

"Who...who are you?" Will asked, coming closer. The woman had long, thick hair that once had been ebony but now was streaked with silver, tied at the nape of her neck.

"I'm Quella. Greenlee came by my place after he left you in the fall. Said I might be needed over here at the time of the Wolf Moon. I can see he was right." She looked into Margaret's eyes. "You are going to be fine, my little one," Quella assured her. "As is your own little one. But we got some mighty work to do comin' on."

Margaret let out a loud wail at that moment, and gush of water ran down her leg and onto the hard dirt floor. The granny woman nodded. "Looks like it's comin' on real fast." She turned to Will and the others. "Men, go fetch buckets of water and lots of wood. Women stay, stoke the fire and heat that water as soon as you can."

They all obeyed as if they were soldiers following the orders of a general. When Will returned with the wood, he saw that Quella had Margaret standing up, walking slowly around the tiny cabin. Esther and Mary were at the fireplace, watching the scene in nothing short of horror.

"It's all right, Mother Esther," Will said, bringing her the armload of wood. "She's a known granny woman, a midwife from over the mountains. Greenlee said she's the one the mountain folk call on for a birthing."

Still, Esther appeared to be appalled. "She...she's an Indian, isn't she?" she whispered.

Until that moment, Will hadn't considered the woman's countenance. But looking at her now, he saw the dark eyes, the high cheekbones, the tawny skin, the hand sewn leather of her dress, and he knew Esther was right. She was Indian. Or half-breed.

Greenlee had told him of the odd, sometime murderous ways of the Indian people. Did he dare entrust the life of his wife and child to this woman? He went to Margaret.

"Do you want me to tell her to go, Margaret? I didn't send for her. I don't know how she knew to come this night." His voice shook slightly, and he was prepared for some kind of violence from the woman, but neither the granny woman nor his wife appeared distraught.

"Please, Will, I think I will be fine now." She grimaced and breathed heavily as another contraction swept through her. Then she said, "I want you to go. Take Da and Mary home. Mam is here with me, and this good woman," she added, smiling slightly at Quella. With that, she stood on tiptoe and kissed Will's lips. "We will let you know when our son, or daughter, is born."

Will left in a daze with a reluctant and somewhat rebellious Mary in tow. "I'm a woman now," she protested. "I want to be with Margaret."

But Will reminded her that Margaret had asked her to leave. "Seems she's not wanting a lot of company while she goes through this."

Fergus had brought water from a nearby branch that fed into the river and was likewise instructed to leave. Together, the three of them made their way to the McKinney cabin. Mary sulked into her room and went back to her bed, fully clothed, just in case she might be called on. Fergus and Will pulled two chairs to the hearth and sat quietly side by side, each lost in his thoughts and fears.

Presently, Fergus rose. "Wait here," he said to Will and went out the door. He returned with a jug that held their first batch of liquid corn from their new homestead. Placing it on the floor between the two chairs, he fetched two tin cups. "I'm thinking maybe we might need a bit of this tonight," he told Will, pouring some of the fiery liquid into each cup.

Jeannette Esther Gordon was born early the following morning, a squalling scrap of a girl that seemed glad to be free of the confined space of her mother's womb. Margaret was exhausted but exhilarated. Esther cried with joy and relief. Mary wasn't sure what to do, so she busied herself making breakfast for the family.

Quella was nowhere to be found.

* * *

May 1754

After the spring planting was done, Will and Fergus, both falling within the age limit of able-bodied men who were by North Carolina colonial law obliged to sign up to serve in the militia if the need arose, rode together into the settlement that was now formally named Salisbury and was the county seat of the newly-formed Rowan County, for a required muster. There was no war, no immediate danger, but Matthew Rowan, the acting governor, had sent word that all precautions should be taken in light of the increasing hostilities between the English and the French.

As much as Will enjoyed the peace of their valley, he sometimes missed being around others in a community such as he'd known in Cross Creek. Here in Salisbury, he found men like himself, settlers who'd come in search of land and a new life and who didn't give a damn for the English. There were Scots-Irish, hailing from the northern provinces of Ireland, Germans, some from Holland and other European countries. They were mostly farmers, merchants, and tradesmen, and unlike Will and his family, most all of them had come into North Carolina from Pennsylvania and Virginia on what they called the Great Wagon Road.

The men gathered on a large open field just outside of town where they were met by a company of provincials, paid military troops, who were in charge of training the locals. They wore blue uniforms with red lining and trim, reminiscent to Will of the hated red coats of the English. He might be required to serve in the local militia, whose job it was to protect their own homes and families, but he would never don a uniform provided by the English.

As the militia men lined up, side by side as directed by the provincial commander, Will accidentally bumped into the man to his left. "Sorry," he said, glancing at the man's face. He appeared to be about Will's age, fair of hair and complexion. Like Will, he was dressed in the manner of the backcountry man.

"No offense taken," the man said. "Guess none of us is used to lining up like them boys over there," he added, pointing at the uniforms. At that moment, the commander of the provincials shouted orders, and for the next few hours, Will, Fergus, and the others marched and drilled together, although Will had to admit they were a rather rag-tag bunch. Each had brought his own weapon, mostly single shot flintlock muskets, and carried a powder horn and shot bag. Unlike the trained provincials, the militia men kept untidy lines and took longer to load and fire their weapons, having no cartridges premeasured with black powder and lead balls.

At the sound of the first shots, Will's skin turned clammy as he remembered that long ago day when the sound of military gunfire meant the death of all he had ever known. He didn't want to appear a coward, but his stomach lurched, and he feared he might be sick. Shooting a deer for food was one thing; shooting people was another. He took a deep breath, garnering control. He thought about his Da, how brave he'd been, how he'd stood up to challenges no matter what, even when it meant dying at Culloden. Drawing a strong image of Alexander Gordon into his mind, and then another of Margaret and their baby, whose lives he might have to defend, Will leveled his rifle and aimed at an invisible target across the meadow. He could, and would, fight for those he loved.

As the muster concluded, the man he'd bumped into came over to him and extended his hand. "I'm Samuel Davidson," he said. "This here's my twin brother, William."

"Will Gordon," he replied, shaking their hands, "and my father-in-law, Fergus McKinney."

"You live near Salisbury?" Samuel asked.

"No. About a day's ride." Will described the location of their farm, along the banks of the Yadkin, and Davidson nodded in approval.

"Sounds like you've stretched the edge of the frontier. We've been here a couple of years, but now I'm itching to move on. Going on to the Catawba River come fall."

The four made their way to a pub and enjoyed a lager brewed by a local German before going their separate ways.

CHAPTER ELEVEN

Later that summer, the Davidson brothers came riding hard into the farmyard, scattering chickens and setting the dogs barking. Margaret hurried out of their cabin, carrying Jeannette on one hip, a musket in the other hand. "Who are you?" she demanded, but Will was out the door right behind her.

"Friends," Will said, taking the gun away. He was glad Margaret had learned to shoot, but sorry she was so brave that she was almost foolhardy. How did she think she could shoot a gun while holding a baby?

"There's been Indians killed not far from here," Samuel said, dismounting. "Thought you folks needed to know."

Will whistled loudly, signaling Fergus to come in from the field and sending the dogs into a frenzy. Esther and Mary came running as well.

"Tell us what's happened," Will said, inviting the men to step into the shade of his small porch and take a seat.

The men related that some Catawbas had come across two Frenchmen and three of their allied Indians not two miles from the Rowan County courthouse and had killed them.

"What are they doing this far south?" Fergus asked, wiping his brow with his sleeve. "I thought all that damned French problem was up north, in Pennsylvania and New York."

"Fergus!" Esther remonstrated automatically. "Your language."

But no one paid attention to her. Will drew Margaret and Jeannette closer. He, too, wanted to know why Frenchmen and northern Indians were in the area.

"Best we can tell," William replied, "they were a scouting party. Probably looking to see what kind of defenses we have around here. Word is, last spring the French ran off some Virginians trying to build a fort at the Forks of the Allegheny on the Ohio and built themselves a fort instead. Duquesne, I believe it's called. They're building forts all up and down the western slopes of the Appalachians, and they're recruiting the Indians to join forces with them against the English."

Will exchanged glances with Fergus. This validated the story told them by Hiram Greenlee, the trader.

Samuel frowned, a deep furrow lining his tanned brow. "I believe, friends, we're going to be caught up in a war between the French and the English, like it or not. I, for one, don't like either of them, and I wish there was some way we could be free from both."

Will closed his eyes. War. *War ain't pretty.* Mr. Simpson's words from long ago echoed in his mind. Was there no place where a man could live and raise a family in peace? "What should we do?" he asked.

"Keep watch. Alert the others who live out here in the backcountry. And keep your weapons handy." Sam Davidson looked straight at Will. "I don't think it's the English or the French we have to worry about most, at least not directly. It's the Indians, especially the northern tribes that they are using as pawns. The French are promising them guns and ammunition and stronger trade agreements than with the English. And," he added, "promising to rid their lands of the hated English."

"And the Indians think the French will be any better?" Fergus snorted. "Those sneaky bastards will move in the minute the English are defeated."

"Fergus!" Esther exclaimed again.

"What about the Catawba, and the Cherokee?" Will asked. "Those closer to us."

"Those two tribes are traditional enemies. The Catawba are friendly. They're the ones that killed the scouting party. The opinion is that they'll remain loyal to the British. But the Cherokee, that's another story."

Will recalled Greenlee's warning that the Cherokee would likely change sides, depending on which country made them the best offer. "Cherokee land's over yonder," Will said, pointing toward the west, "over the mountains."

"Not to their minds," William replied. "That's where they have villages, but they've always hunted these lands. They've been seen this side of the mountains lately, and if the French put a bounty on English scalps, which I've heard of them doing, and the Cherokee take them up on it, it's possible they could show up around here."

At this Esther fainted. Mary barely caught her before she hit the ground. "See now, you've gone and scared Mam," Mary said crossly, waving a kerchief over her mother's pale face.

The visitors rose immediately and made ready to leave. "Sorry, ma'am. We didn't mean to, but in truth, we should all be scared, or at least vigilant in these times."

Sam turned to Will and Fergus. "If your women feel in need of better protection, you might want to take them to the Moravians over in Bethabara."

Will and Fergus walked the pair to where their horses grazed and bade them goodbye, thanking them for bringing the news, as bad as it was.

"Tomorrow, we'll ride to the Patersons and the Murreys and let them know," Will said. "But there's others down river too far for us to go and leave our place unprotected."

"We're headed that way, and over to the Broad River as well. Heard there's some good hunting to be had there." Sam grinned. "Can't let the Cherokee have all the good game."

* * *

The second summer had seen sufficient rain, which brought a bounty of corn and wheat in the fields, some of which Fergus and Will turned into their liquid commodity. By late summer, Margaret, Esther and Mary had put up all the garden vegetables that could be stored for winter. Potatoes were dug and packed into a root cellar. The cow continued to give ample milk, and the chickens flourished in their new henhouse. Life was not easy, Will allowed, but neither was it unduly hard or unpleasant. Just different from anything he'd ever dreamed of. Happier than he ever thought he could be, in spite of this Indian threat.

So far, no more Indians had been sighted in their area, but as a precaution, Will and Fergus bought additional guns and ammunition and made sure all three women knew how to use them. Mary refused at first, but gave in when Will asked her, "What would you do to protect yourself if we're off in the fields or at muster or something, and Indians came around to attack you?" That gave her pause, and reluctantly, she took her shooting lessons, surprising everyone that she was actually quite a good marksman.

News of just such an attack arrived shortly thereafter when Hiram Greenlee returned to the farm with a wagon loaded with deerskins. He took Will and Fergus aside, out of earshot of the women. "There's been an Indian raid over on the Broad River," he told them. "Nobody knows what tribe they were from, but they think they were under French influence."

Will and Fergus exchanged glances. The Broad was further to the west, but nothing said the raiders couldn't make their way to the Yadkin. "What happened?"

"Killed sixteen settlers and took another ten captive." He spat out the tobacco he was chewing. "I'd rather be dead than captured by any Indian. I've seen firsthand how they sometimes torture their captives before finally killing them." He shuddered.

Will had a sudden image of Indians attacking their beautiful farm, killing or stealing away his family, maybe burning the cabins. He closed his eyes, feeling helpless. They could and would fight back, but there were only five of them, isolated on the frontier. He doubted they could overcome a larger band of raiders.

"What about the provincials?" Fergus asked. "Why aren't they out here if they know something like this is happening?"

"Got to ask Rowan about that, I guess. What I understand from the traders I know, North Carolina soldiers have been sent up to Virginia and on north to fight the French and Indians up there. Guess they didn't reckon on something like this happening out here."

Will nodded. "Sounds like we're pretty much on our own for now," he said, at first angry at not receiving protection from the colony but then quickly realizing he'd gotten exactly what he'd wanted—freedom. He and Fergus both had agreed that living free out here on the frontier was their goal. Free from landlords and laws and rules and politics and kings. Answering only to themselves, and God.

But clearly, that freedom came with a price. He hoped they would be spared any Indian encounters, but he was no fool.

The trader made ready to leave. "I'll be spending tonight down the river a-ways. Going into Salisbury tomorrow to provision for the ride on down to Charlestown. They've built that city back up, you know, after that hurricane a few years back, but they're just now recovering their crops. I'll be making a pretty penny with what I'm taking with me from here."

"We have corn we can sell you if you're interested," Fergus said. "And wheat. We have more than plenty for our own needs."

They bartered with the old trader, corn and wheat for skins that the women would make into coats for winter, and salt from the mines over the mountains. Fergus gave him a jug of corn whiskey as a gift, which pleased Greenlee immensely. "By the way," he said, hiding the jug beneath a layer of hides, "if Indians come your way, don't let 'em know you got this. They'll take it and drink it down fast as anything, and then they really get mean."

When at last Greenlee went on his way, Fergus and Will took a long walk, surveying the edge of their land, eyes seeking the enemy in the forest. "We've heard all this before," Will said. "Greenlee warned us last year. Then the Davidsons. Now this. We need to consider what to do."

After a long conversation, they returned, and the family gathered at the McKinney's cabin. "I never meant to put us in harm's way," Fergus said in a low tone. "But I fear we are there. We have a choice. We can leave this farm and head back to Cross Creek and start again. We've done it before. We can do it again. It would be safer there."

To everyone's amazement, Esther said, "No! I won't be moved again. Enough is enough."

"But Mam," Mary said, "what if the Indians come?"

"Let them. I'll shoot to kill. We all will. And if we lose, well, we'll be in God's hands then. Better that than all this hard work going for naught. Besides," she turned and smiled at Fergus. "I've grown used to being out here. I love this valley. It's beautiful. We've made do so far. We can make it better each year."

Will was astounded at her turn of heart. He wasn't sure she'd ever become comfortable with their outback life, and he'd figured Esther and Mary would jump at Fergus's offer to leave a place where their lives might be in danger.

Margaret spoke up. "I agree. But Will, is there nothing we can do to seek aid from the colony?"

That night, by lantern light, after Jeannette was settled and Margaret was in bed, Will sat at the table and drafted a letter. "Dear Mr. Rowan..."

CHAPTER TWELVE

In November, all militia men were called to an urgent muster in Salisbury. This time, Margaret, Jeannette, Mary, and Esther accompanied the men, none of the family wanting the women to be left alone and unprotected on the farm. The women used the opportunity to purchase supplies of household goods, cloth, sewing needs, salt, sugar, and coffee. The men reported for duty.

When the militia men were gathered, they were greeted by an imposing, handsome young man, Captain Hugh Waddell of the British provincial army, astride a gray mount. "Good day, gentlemen," he said, "and thank you for coming." Will found his demeanor strong yet amenable. It seemed odd that such a personage would be present at the muster of backcountry men. What was up?

"I greet you on behalf of your new governor, Arthur Dobbs, and the president of the Colonial Council, Matthew Rowan. Both of these gentlemen have received letters from some among you, including militia officer John Clark and one named Will Gordon, outlining the atrocities committed along the Broad River by an Indian raiding party and requesting aid from the colony for protection of these far western counties."

At this, Will's face reddened. He had told no one about writing that letter. He'd crept out of the cabin that night, found Greenlee camped by the river, and asked that he find a way to send it in Salisbury, never really believing it would be read by Rowan.

"In response, the governor has assigned me to head a Frontier Company of one hundred provincial soldiers to serve as rangers," the captain told them. "We will be riding and scouting throughout the region, with the intention of preventing this kind of tragedy and securing the homes and families of those of you who so bravely have chosen to enlarge the settlement of western North Carolina. He also plans to build a fort further to the west of here for protection."

At this, a spontaneous huzzah arose from the crowd, and Will received several nudges from some of those who knew him. "You wrote the governor?" Fergus asked in a loud whisper.

Will nodded. "Margaret asked if there wasn't something I could do to help us," he replied. "It was all I knew to do. I never expected to hear anything." But secretly, he was pleased that perhaps his simple letter had made a difference. He was anxious to meet this Captain Waddell.

After the exercises and drills that were supervised by some of Waddell's rangers, the militia dispersed, and Will, Fergus, the Davidson brothers, the Paterson men, and Gil Murrey retired to the inn where some of them were staying and were joined there by the women in their families. The news about the new ranger patrols spread like wildfire through the small settlement, and at last the beleaguered and frightened frontier families found some measure of hope in being able to remain on their farms.

"This is all good," Fergus said to those gathered for the evening meal that night. "But we should make sure we have covered all possible means of protection. Tomorrow, on our way home, well, not exactly on the way, but as a short detour, our family will be visiting Bethabara. We've heard the Moravians are willing to offer shelter to other settlers should the need arise."

This was the first Will had heard of Fergus's plan, but he agreed it was a good idea. The Moravians were considered by other settlers to be an insular group, a colony formed by Bishop Spangenberg to serve the religious doctrine of these immigrants who had obtained a large tract of land from Lord Granville. But upon meeting them and being greeted warmly by the bishop and others, Will discovered a group of people who lived a simple communal life and who generously offered food and shelter to anyone in need.

"We are all God's children," Spangenberg said in English but with a deep German accent as he showed them the new compound. "There is no one we would turn away."

"Even the Indians?" Mary blurted. Fergus glared at her, but the bishop only smiled.

"Even the Indians. They, too, are God's children."

His equanimity put Will in mind of what Greenlee had told him about the Indians and their belief that the Great Spirit had put them on this land, that it was for all of His children to use, but not to own. How had they come so far away from their spiritual beliefs that they would murder and scalp those innocents down on the Broad River? But the answer was clear. Those children of God, or the Great Spirit, or Whoever was in control, who came from Europe, Moravians included, wanted to own, not share, the land. He thought, too, of Greenlee's statement that what the Indians weren't given, they would take. Were they simply trying to take back their right to what the Great Spirit had given them?

Will's mind was overwhelmed by this thinking, and he refocused his attention on what the bishop was telling them as they walked through the small lanes of the village. These industrious immigrants had already built houses and planted a community garden. Esther and Margaret were particularly interested in their physic garden in which they grew many medicinal herbs. Will and Fergus were more interested in the possible protection the community might offer their family.

"We understand, sir," he addressed the bishop, "that you are willing to offer sanctuary to any who seek refuge from the Indian attacks that seem to have increased as of late. But, and I ask this with respect, your village seems as vulnerable to them as our isolated farms, other than the number you have living here to serve in its defense."

Spangenberg just smiled. "The Indians will not harm us, son," he replied patiently.

Will frowned. "Why not?" He wondered if this man thought the Great Spirit was going to look after them.

"The Indians are not our enemy," the bishop answered. "We have fed those who have passed our way and were in need, the same as we would do for you." He laughed. "I hear they call this a place of large Dutchi and good bread."

On their way back to the farm, Will rode ahead, troubled and confused. His loathing of the English had not abated over the years since Culloden, and yet he was grateful for Hugh Waddell and his rangers, who he hoped would protect them from the Indians. He recalled Greenlee's comments about the Indians, and a small part of him could understand their anger at having the whites encroach upon land their people had occupied apparently for centuries.

And yet, they had signed agreements allowing settlers to move on westward. What was it Greenlee had said—treaties made, treaties broken. What treaties were broken, and by whom? But he knew it was the English. White settlers hungry for land.

* * *

They returned to find their cabins intact and their livestock undisturbed, and Will began to relax a little. He hadn't realized how tense and worried he'd become. Still, one of the first things he did upon arriving was check to see that all guns were at the ready and ammunition easily available.

Early the next morning, he was awakened by screaming, and he grabbed his rifle as he headed out the door. The screaming didn't stop, and it was coming from the henhouse. Margaret was right behind him, hatchet in hand. Both were barefoot and still in their nightclothes. They approached the henhouse cautiously, when suddenly the door burst open and a small black and white striped creature dashed out and across the garden directly in front of them, headed for the woods. Behind him he left a pungent stench, and Mary, who had been gathering eggs in the henhouse, was doused in it.

They ran to the door and pulled her outside, still screaming her head off and crying. And stinking. "Good lord," Will said, holding his breath and keeping Mary at arm's length. "A skunk."

Margaret took more pity on her sister and attempted to embrace her, but she gagged and backed away. Fergus and Esther came out of their cabin when the commotion started, but they, too, kept their distance. Then Mary sank to the ground and vomited.

"We have to get her cleaned up," Margaret said, taking her sister's hand and pulling her to her feet. "I'll take her to the river. Mam, bring some lye soap and her other dress."

Will and Fergus opened the door wide and all the chickens flew out in a wave of the skunk's odor. "Guess they'll run free for awhile," Fergus commented, and then he broke into one of his hearty laughs. "Don't tell

Mary I laughed," he said to Will. "But it had to be poor Mary who got skunked. She's so afraid of everything. Now she'll likely not want to go in to gather the eggs."

Will did see the humor in it, although he knew Margaret would give him a round scolding if he let on, so he bit his lips and went back to get dressed. The sun was well up by the time the women returned from the river, both shivering. Mary's hair dripped onto her second-best dress, and she cried continually. Esther took her to their cabin, but left her on the front porch, while Margaret came toward Will.

"Did she clean up all right?" he asked.

Margaret let out a long breath. "Well, almost. But...we're going to have to cut her hair off. There's no getting the smell out of it."

Life on the frontier, Will thought. There was more than one kind of enemy out here. He had a terrible but fleeting thought. Mary was going to lose her pretty hair, at least temporarily. It was like the skunk had scalped her. The analogy was too awful to even consider, and Will quickly let it go.

Chapter Thirteen

Yadkin River Valley, Autumn 1756

Will and several of his neighbors left before dawn to ride to the newly constructed fort, named Fort Dobbs after the governor of North Carolina. Fergus remained to defend the farm if needed. The men being part of the militia of Rowan and Anson Counties had been called to muster at the new fort, and Will was apprehensive about the reason behind the summons.

Fort Dobbs was an impressive fortification, situated on an open plain near the Fourth Fork of the Yadkin River. It was built of sturdy oak logs and stood three stories into the sky. A British flag fluttered in the breeze from a pole nearly as tall as the building. As they approached, they saw others gathering for the muster. Will looked for the Davidson brothers, but didn't see them.

The riders were greeted by Captain Hugh Waddell, who had been appointed by the governor to build and garrison the fort with his company of provincial rangers. "Welcome, gentlemen," he said, ushering them inside the walls that were covered by a sizable roof. Daylight entered only through the openings that served as portals for muskets, and the interior gloom was barely offset by the light of lanterns.

Once inside, the militia men were given hot coffee and told to stand at ease. "Thank you for coming, gentlemen," Captain Waddell said. "This invitation to muster was issued by Governor Dobbs, who is committed to preserving the safety of those of you here on the frontier's edge."

At this a murmur rustled through the gathering. All of them knew that despite the efforts of Waddell's rangers, Indian raids, robberies, and murders continued to occur in the area.

Waddell continued. "You've been summoned because...well, others of our North Carolina regiments have been sent north to fight the French and their northern Indian allies. The war has gone badly, frankly, and the colony's resources are stretched to the limit. We asked you to come here to encourage you to join our efforts in safeguarding this outpost and the surrounding territory if the need arises. The forty-six provincials we have here are simply not enough to get the job done."

"How badly goes the war, sir?" Jake, George Paterson's oldest son, asked. "And how does that affect our lives here?"

"To be frank, the British lost the fight to recapture Fort Duquesne last year, and since then have lost Fort Oswego to the French, which was to be the base of operations for attacks against three French forts critical to their supply lines. Other offensives have been only marginally successful."

Waddell began to pace, and Will could tell this was difficult for him. It seemed the British might face defeat, and Waddell, a close friend of Governor Dobbs, was a strong supporter of the king.

"How this might affect you and your families is this...if the French are successful in the north, there will be nothing to prevent them from moving southward and attacking British colonies, including North and South Carolina and Virginia. Since they are using Indians in their fight, we will likely see an increase in these raids, perhaps an all-out war at some point."

The room grew so silent Will could hear himself breathe. "Are the Cherokees aligned with the French?" he asked at last.

"Not formally. No, in fact, the governors of all three of these colonies have been working with the chiefs of the Cherokee and the Catawba tribes to seek peace. It is important to maintain our strong trade relationships with them, and that they remain loyal to our cause."

"I expect they might change sides, depending on which offers them the most guns, ammunition, and trade goods," said a man in the crowd that Will recognized as his neighbor, Daniel Boone.

"Unfortunately, that is true, Mr. Boone. You of all people understand their nature. That is why we are working hard to maintain their good will. Despite these intermittent attacks, the tribes, especially the Cherokee, provide a barrier of sorts between you settlers here on the frontier and the French, should they encroach." Waddell took a swallow of his coffee, then added, "Governor Dobbs has sent me explicit instructions that we should try to maintain the peace if at all possible. We are to report any abuses by members of their tribes directly to the chiefs in person and ask that the delinquents be turned over to us for prosecution, rather than strike out in revenge."

"What if they refuse?" Will asked, growing increasingly ill at ease.

"We are to request them to warn their hunters and warriors not to molest any English who have settled here, and that if they don't, we will be obliged to repel force with force." He paused, then looked up gravely at the men who stood before him. "That's where you come in."

Following the briefing, those gathered were asked to participate in a drill on the grounds outside the fort. Most of the men obliged, but a number of them chose to leave. Will overheard some comments such as, "I'll fight my own fight, not with the bloody British." But as the men from their valley rode home, their conversation was somber. They had all agreed to serve with Waddell if they were called to become active in the militia in the fight against the Indians, but only in defense of their lives and property. They were uneasy that the British might call them up for duty in other parts of the country, and that they were not willing to do.

* * *

1757-1758

Word spread among the settlers on the Yadkin River that Captain Waddell, now Major Waddell, had been ordered to take his troops from Fort Dobbs to fight in Pennsylvania, leaving the western frontier exposed once again to Indian attacks. Will and his neighbors were implored to join the provincials in this fight, but they were unwilling to leave their families and their land unprotected.

Many of the settlers, frightened by the increasing attacks, some by Indians returning from serving in a mercenary capacity in General Washington's army, deserted their land and fled east to greater safety. Even the peaceful Moravians whose faith prevented them from serving in the military had built a second stockade around their water mill and strengthened the palisade built earlier. Refugees flocked there for protection until all their cabins were filled.

Again, Will and Fergus conferred with their families on what to do, and again, the decision was made to stay. "Surely this can't go on forever," Fergus remarked, but Will heard the doubt behind his words.

CHAPTER FOURTEEN

Yadkin River Valley, April 1759

"Y**ou** go on ahead with Mary and Jeannette," Margaret said to Will. "They're excited about the birthday party and won't want to miss a minute. Da and Mam and I will be along as soon as we're done with a few chores."

"There's no hurry," Will countered. "The girls can wait."

But Margaret was adamant. She brought a casserole in a crockery dish from their kitchen shed and stashed it beneath the seat of the wagon. "Go. Take this to Mrs. Paterson. She'll be waiting for it to share as part of the dinner. I'm sure all the Patersons will be waiting, especially Jake," she said, lowering her voice. "Truth is, that's why Mary's so eager to go. Haven't you noticed they have eyes for each other?" she added with a knowing smile. "Reminds me of us not so long ago."

Will grinned. Indeed, he did remember their courting days, and how much he'd wanted to spend his time with Margaret. He understood now why Mary had been preening and prancing around anxiously all morning, so he gave a whistle and signaled for her to bring Jeannette and get in the wagon. "Don't be too long," he admonished Margaret as he bent to kiss her.

"We'll be right along on the horses," she promised.

The Patersons held the land adjacent to the McKinney farm just to the north, about two miles away along a road the families had cleared out of the forest that lay between them. They'd built a grist mill on the river that served the local farm families. George and Emily Paterson were of similar age as Fergus and Esther, and they had two sons, Jacob, who was called Jake, and Josiah, known as Joe. Jake was turning twenty today, and Mary was now eighteen. Will wondered if there was going to be more to celebrate today than a birthday.

When they arrived, they were greeted by the group gathered for this special occasion, including the Murreys and two other families who had settled on the western bank of the river. The young people were dashing about, and Will saw Jake help Mary down from the wagon with a look in his eyes that left no doubt he was in love with her. Will took the dish to Emily, explaining that the rest of their clan would be along shortly.

He took a tin cup from those lined up on the porch rail for the guests to use and poured himself some of the sassafras tea Emily had in a nearby pitcher. He turned and watched all the children at play, his own Jeannette being the youngest but trying her best to participate in the games. He felt a pang of regret that he and Margaret had no more children. Neither could explain it. She had conceived Jeannette so easily, and both had wanted a large family. Will couldn't ignore the niggle at the back of his mind, wondering if somehow that Indian woman, Quella, hadn't cast a spell over Margaret, rendering her barren.

An hour passed, and then two, and finally Emily came over to Will. "Do you suppose they'll be coming soon? We should ring the dinner bell now. Everyone else is here, and I can see by the way they're eyeing the table, they are hungry."

Under a large tree in their yard, George had set up a makeshift table made of long planks of wood supported by wooden braces. It was covered with a colorful cloth probably woven by Emily, and laden with dishes the families had brought to share.

"Go ahead," Will told her. "I'm sure they wouldn't want to hold up the party." But even as the dinner bell rang, an alarm went off in the pit of his stomach. They should have been here long ago, he believed. He had unhitched his horse from the wagon, and now fetched and mounted it. "You children stay and play," he told Mary and Jeannette. "I'm going to find the laggards who are going to miss a great feast if they don't appear soon."

With that, he turned the horse back down the road, riding at a trot at first, but then spurring the animal into a gallop. Something was wrong. It wasn't like them to be this late to a gathering he knew they were all looking forward to.

He whistled as he approached. "Margaret! Fergus! Esther! What's taking you so long?" His horse whinnied and shied as they neared the first cabin, the one shared by his family. The place was eerily silent. Even the birds held their tongues. The hair on the back of his neck bristled, and he dismounted with his gun in hand.

He spotted Fergus first, lying face down at the edge of the field. Running to him, he saw immediately that he was dead of a gunshot wound in his chest, and that his rich, red hair had been taken. Fear as strong as what he'd felt at Culloden clutched his stomach, and he leaned over and wretched.

The Indians had come at last.

Panicked now, he dashed to the side of his cabin where the kitchen and gardens lay, and his world came crashing down. Both Margaret and Esther lay among the rows of vegetables they'd planted, their bodies stabbed and slashed, their scalps removed. Blood ran thick into the earth beneath them.

"No!" he cried out. "Noooo!" He ran to Margaret, hoping to find some sign of life, but her face was ashen and cold, as was Esther's. He closed his eyes against the horror, and then he began to shake with tears and rage. He crumpled to the ground, covering Margaret's inert figure with his body. This couldn't be. His beloved, spritely Margaret killed by savages. His family was dead. His dreams, as well, had now turned to ashes.

George Paterson and Gil Murrey found him there some time later, still covering Margaret's body with his own, his tears dried, but his heart bleeding as if he'd been stabbed as well.

The neighbors managed to pull Will to his feet, and one found some corn whiskey to restore his senses. Leaving him temporarily to recover on his porch, they looked around the farmyard and discovered that the horses had been stolen and the livestock slaughtered. There was no sign of Indians other than a feathered spear that had been embedded into the side of his cabin.

"They're likely still nearby," George said. "We'd better all get back to our place and decide what to do."

"Their bodies," Will said weakly. "We must bury them. Mary and Jeannette must not see this."

And so, the three dug shallow graves on the higher ground above the cabins and placed his adopted parents and his beautiful wife into the rich, loamy soil of North Carolina.

* * *

"We must leave now!" Emily Paterson screamed, nearly hysterical after hearing what had happened. "They're here! They're among us somewhere out there," she pointed toward the west. "Quick! Sons, gather what you can into the wagons. I'll not stay another moment in this godforsaken place." And then she broke down into unrelenting sobs.

Will looked somberly at George and Gil. "She's right," he said. "We should have heeded the warnings before now and left." His words sounded lame, but he didn't know what else to say, or do.

Mary and Jeannette were crying, and Will gathered them close to his side. "I'm taking my girls to Bethabara. Nobody's garrisoned at Fort Dobbs anymore. We're pretty much defenseless unless we find safety in numbers and behind strong walls."

"I heard a lot of folks have already sought shelter there," Gil Murrey said, holding his wife and young son to his sides as well. "They've built a couple of palisades to keep the Indians out."

Will recalled Spangenberg's statement that Indians were God's children too, and he wondered if he was still of that mind. Bethabara was about twenty miles from their farms, and it was late in the day, but the settlers hastened to leave. "They could come in the night," one of the women said. "There's nothing I need from our place that's important enough to risk our lives."

Will hitched his horse back to his wagon, fetched the crockery dish and filled it with water for the journey, and he, Mary and Jeannette, all three stunned and shaken, joined the sad parade of wagons, horses, and settlers headed to what they hoped would be safety. It was to be a long night.

At Bethabara they were greeted by the Moravians with food and words of comfort and shown to a space enclosed by tall, spiked rails that surrounded the mill. When Will spoke with the bishop later that day, he learned that the good man had indeed changed his perception of the natives somewhat.

"They've killed innocents like your family," he said, and tears welled in his eyes. "So many have died, I can no longer offer them the comfort and forgiveness of God. They are murderers, and they are likely to come to our back door as well."

Other settlers trickled in over the course of the next few days, causing such crowding within the palisades that it reminded Will of the crowded conditions on board the *Orion*. Except these refugees had nothing to look forward to, and nothing but grief in their hearts. He learned that his family was just one among many who had been massacred along the Yadkin and Catawba rivers.

"Warriors from Settico," he heard a familiar voice say and turned to see Hiram Greenlee among the newly arrived. "I was there last month, and what I heard turned my knees to jelly," he spoke to a group of men who'd gathered outside the palisade. "It's the damned French again, this time stirred up the Creeks who came to Settico and taunted the Cherokee, saying they were cowards for not seeking revenge against the English."

"Revenge for what?" someone asked.

"Bad business all the way around. Seems Cherokee warriors who were promised payment for fighting with the English against the French and the northern Indians up in Virginia didn't get what they thought they were owed. On their way home, up in Virginia, they stole horses and raided settlers' homes. Understandably, the settlers have fought back. Lots have been killed on both sides, and the Cherokees up in Settico, the ones who did the fightin', are real riled up. And then here comes the Creeks, paid by the French, to stir 'em up even more."

"But why would they come this far east and attack us?" Gil Murrey wanted to know.

"They know Fort Dobbs is basically defenseless," Greenlee replied. "The settlers to the south have Fort Prince George to protect them, and none of the warriors is interested in returning to Virginia at the moment. So, it's my guess they figured you was easy pickings."

Will shook his head. "Was this their blood revenge for Cherokees killed up in Virginia?"

"I would assume so. It's their way, you know, sort of a Biblical kind of revenge, an eye for an eye and all that."

In his mind's eye, Will saw the mutilated body of his wife, the heartless murder and scalping of innocent people, and he vowed revenge of his own. Henceforth he would kill any Indian he saw. He didn't care what tribe they might be from. An Indian, in his mind, was an Indian, and they had taken from him most everything and everyone he ever cared for in his life.

He strode away from the group, trying to control his rage and was met by Jeannette running out of the palisade and up the dirt road toward him.

"Da," she cried and flung herself against his large body. "Da." And then she cried so hard it broke his anger. Together, they sat on a log on the side of the road and wept.

CHAPTER FIFTEEN

Hugh Waddell, now a colonel in the North Carolina colonial army, arrived within a short time with two companies of provincials to re-garrison Fort Dobbs and patrol the North Carolina frontier. Too little too late was Will's opinion, but George said better late than never.

George became Will's best friend during their weeks at Bethabara, sharing mutual grief, fear, and anger. They dared not return to their farms, as Indian scalping parties were known to still roam the region. Will was frustrated at not having a means to seek retribution, but George counseled him to bide his time.

"Your family needs you here," he said, indicating the direction of the small plot of ground now occupied by Mary and Jeannette. There were no cabins for shelter within the palisade, but they'd erected a canvas cover under which they slept on blankets on the ground. They, too, had lost so much.

Will had to admit George was right. They needed him here. But still, Will grew restless and hungered for a way to fight back against a foe that remained faceless, but cruel beyond belief. He had no appetite for aiding the English, but the garrison at Fort Dobbs offered him the opportunity to take some action.

"I'm going to ride over to Dobbs and see what's happening," he told Mary and Jeannette one night. "I want the two of you to stay here, where you'll be protected." He stopped short of saying they'd be safe. He didn't believe anywhere in North Carolina was safe at the moment.

"Mary, you've been of great comfort to Jeannette, and I want you to know how much I appreciate your bravery."

Mary, who'd never been particularly brave, batted her tear-laden eyes. "I've no choice, Will, but to be brave. But the truth is, I'm terrified. I want to leave this land and go home."

Will nodded. This was not unexpected, but he didn't know how to help her. "I understand. I wish now we'd left when we talked about it years ago. But who was to know all this would happen?"

Jeannette snuggled up to her father. "Take me with you, Da," she implored.

Will tousled her hair. "When you're older, I'll teach you how to shoot a gun."

"And I'll kill those bad Indians," she said, holding her arms as if shouldering a gun.

A lot of good teaching Margaret and Esther to shoot had done. Neither of them had a gun at hand when they were murdered. Will wondered if the Indians had stolen the weapons or if they were still in his cabin. He hadn't returned home since that horrible day. Figured he might never return. Let some other fool have the farm when they came across it deserted.

Gil Murrey had decided to take his family back to Cross Creek and had left earlier. So Will, George, and George's two sons rode out of Bethabara the following morning. Before leaving, Will had extracted a promise from Mary that she would care for Jeannette as if she were her own child. "Margaret would want it so," he said, and Mary nodded.

* * *

At Fort Dobbs, Will and the others joined the militia unit from Rowan County and volunteered to serve in whatever capacity Waddell needed to secure the North Carolina frontier from the ravages of the Cherokee. To his surprise, however, they were ordered to join the governor of South Carolina, Lyttleton, against the Cherokee. At this, many of the men reneged on their commitment, saying they wouldn't leave their families exposed to danger such as they faced in North Carolina.

In the end, a separate company was raised to support the South Carolina war against the Cherokee, but it was too late. Lyttleton had managed to sign a peace treaty, and Waddell released the company. Will was among the few who chose to stay and patrol the region. "We're all that stands between our people and the Indians," he told George, who'd decided to return to Bethabara.

That winter, Will did return to the Moravian village for a visit, to spend Christmas with Jeannette and Mary, and to celebrate Jeannette's sixth birthday in January. Mary and Jake had become engaged and were married by the Moravian bishop in the small church as snowflakes began to fall. Jeannette had grown a foot, it seemed to Will, and he regretted having missed watching his only child growing up. But he reminded himself that she was alive, and he would do everything in his power to protect her so she could continue to grow up. It was his only consolation for being absent from her for so long.

* * *

Fort Dobbs, North Carolina, February 1760

"Indians in sight!" called a lookout from the upper story of Fort Dobbs. Will and the rest of the small garrison grabbed their muskets and hurried to the center of the wooden enclosure that comprised the only fort on the western frontier of North Carolina.

"I need volunteers to scout around here, see if you can find them, or see signs that might indicate their numbers," Colonel Waddell said to the troops. Will immediately stepped forward, along with four others including his neighbor, Daniel Boone. They cautiously emerged from the protection of the fort, guns at ready. It was a gray day with a brisk, cold wind.

After searching the woods and along the nearby river, they returned emptyhanded, but later that night, they were alarmed by a loud noise outside. This time Waddell himself led a small party to investigate, ordering the remaining soldiers to stay within the fort, lest this be a trick to lure them all out to their deaths. Will was among those with Waddell, walking slowly through the night, listening for sounds that would betray the enemy.

"If we're attacked," Waddell said, "hold your fire until they've exhausted their first round, then fire at my command."

Not three hundred yards from the fort, about sixty warriors emerged from the darkness, yelling and screaming their war cries.

"Hold your fire," Waddell commanded again. A volley of bullets whizzed through the air, one of them striking a soldier next to him. Will had no time to help the man, as the Indians continued to approach, armed now only with tomahawks. Will's finger twitched on his trigger, and his heart pounded as they came nearer and nearer. He could see their eyes and the black war paint on their faces. What was Waddell thinking? But then, he heard the Colonel call, "Now! Shoot now!" and a volley erupted from the soldiers' guns, cutting down the Indians at near point-blank range.

"Fall back," Waddell shouted, and the small group retreated to the fort, which had come under attack from another direction. Will reached for the outstretched arm of the wounded man, dragged him to his feet, and helped him back to safety. Inside the fort, he turned the soldier, Private Fitzgibbons, who was in the regular British army, over to the medical doctor and returned to take up a position and began to fire at the invaders.

Will fought alongside Waddell and ducked when a bullet shattered the officer's musket, tearing it from his hand. Before long, however, the fort held strong, and the Indians ceased their attack. The men stood watch the rest of the night, anticipating a second assault. But by dawn, there was no sign of the attackers.

At daybreak, the men left the fort and searched the areas where the fighting had taken place. "We must have killed about a dozen, probably wounded more," Waddell estimated, although no bodies were found immediately. He also saw that six of his horses were missing. "Probably used them to carry off the dead," he surmised.

Will came across the body of one dead Indian lying face up in the winter grass. He was a young man, with the black paint worn by Cherokee warriors streaked across his cheeks. "Guess they couldn't find this one in the night to haul away," he said, staring at the corpse in fascination. It was the first hostile Indian he'd seen close up, and he wanted to imprint the image in his memory, to help him hold onto the anger at what this man, or his tribe, had done to Margaret and her parents.

"Not much there to scalp, is there?" one of the other soldiers remarked as he joined will to look at the dead man. Cherokees were noted for shaving their heads, leaving only a small tuft at the top, adorned with feathers and beads.

Will was sickened at the thought of the barbarous practice of taking scalps, and he turned away. "Guess we ought to see what the Colonel wants us to do with him."

The garrison suffered one dead, a young man not much more than a boy, and two wounded. One of the wounded had been scalped. "He'll not make it," Waddell said sadly as they moved the man into a bed and tended him as best they could. He died that night.

Will went up to the highest point in the fort and peered out of one of the small square musket holes. He thought about that young boy who'd been killed, and his mind raced back to Culloden as if it were yesterday. That could have been him, back then. What if he'd been killed that day? he mused. What would he have missed?

Margaret. Jeannette. Those warm, happy days on the farms, both in Cross Creek and on the Yadkin. The love of a family. The music and dancing. The satisfaction of raising crops from soil rich and fertile. All this he treasured in his heart, and he wondered sadly what that dead boy would miss.

The attack on Fort Dobbs had failed, but Indians continued to roam the countryside, terrorizing and murdering the few settlers who'd chosen to remain in their homes. Will became uneasy at their close proximity to Bethabara. Would they attack that settlement as well? Or had Spangenberg's "good bread" bought him some protection? Having witnessed the savagery of these barbarians, Will doubted it.

Asking permission for a few days of leave, Will decided to return to his family and friends at Bethabara. What he found was shocking. Supplies had been decimated, many had fallen ill, and they were freezing in the winter's cold with little shelter available. Jeannette spotted her father as he entered the compound and ran to him. She looked tired and disheveled, her golden red hair in tangles and her clothing ragged. But to his eyes, she was beautiful.

"My darling girl," he said, sweeping her into his arms.

She nestled into his shoulder and began to cry. "I thought you were dead," she sobbed.

It hadn't occurred to Will to try to send word back here after the Indian attack.

"Now, now," he said in an attempt to comfort her, but other words failed him, and so he just held her tight.

Mary and Jake found them a few minutes later and rejoiced that he'd returned to them. "We didn't know what to think," Mary said, breathless. "The Indians are so close by we can see their campfires at night. We thought maybe the fort had fallen."

At that moment, the sound of a loud bell ringing split the air, and Will jumped involuntarily. "What's that?"

"The bell on the church. They ring it every hour. It means different things at different times," Mary said, and Jake added, "Mainly it means that the Indians are afraid of it, and it keeps them away."

That night, Will, Mary, Jake, the Patersons and a few other families sat together in quiet conversation.

"We've decided to leave the frontier," George told the group, taking Emily's hand and giving it a squeeze. "We don't know how much longer this war will go on, or even if the Cherokee will leave settlers in peace after the English and French have settled their differences."

Mary clasped her hands and brought them to her chest. "Oh, Father George, that is wonderful news!" But then she turned to her young husband. "Jake? Do you agree?"

But before he could answer, Will broke in. "It is for the best, George, and I will help you. But Mary and Jake, will you take Jeannette with you and keep her safe?"

They looked at each other, then at Will, and Mary said, "Will, we want to adopt her."

Will felt the blood drain from his face. He thought about it for a minute, then replied, "I cannot allow that, Mary. She's...she's all the blood kin I have left. I will send money when I can for her keep, but I cannot give her up to you."

Mary started to object, but Jake laid his hand on her arm. "We understand, Will. And we will continue to care for Jeannette as if she were our own. But know that if the time ever comes that you wish us to adopt her, we will. For now, we think it best if we move back east."

"Will you go with us, Will?" George asked, almost pleading. "We've been together for so long, through thick and thin, as they say. Won't you come along and care for Jeannette yourself?"

Will was torn, but somewhere deep inside, he knew he had to find some way to assuage the anger in his heart, to fill the emptiness that had become his constant companion. He'd thought he could never kill another human being after the massacre at Culloden, even the English that he continued to hate. But the atrocities that the Indians had visited upon his family had changed him. It was as if he'd become a different man, one not only capable of killing, but eager to do so.

"I will accompany you back east and see you installed in a new place," he said after a time. "But I have unfinished business here on the frontier, and until that's settled, I will know no peace."

CHAPTER SIXTEEN

Fort Prince George, South Carolina, May 1761

Will had returned to Fort Dobbs in late summer after seeing his daughter and the other families settled near Corbinton, a tiny settlement east of Salisbury. He'd stayed long enough to help the Patersons locate on a farm near a river and construct a mill similar to the one they'd left behind in the Yadkin Valley. He'd been sorely tempted to remain in the relative peace and safety of the area, but images of the slaughter the Indians had wreaked on his family wouldn't let him be, and he knew he had devils he must deal with first.

At Fort Dobbs, he'd learned that South Carolina had taken military action against the Cherokee the previous summer, but with only moderate success. "Why doesn't North Carolina take some action like that?" he asked Waddell one night at mess. Will and some of the others were volunteer rangers now, based out of Fort Dobbs and scouting the western territories of the state in an attempt to end the Indian raids there. They, too, had met with only moderate success, and the raids continued.

"No money to support such an operation," was Waddell's blunt answer. "And...political in-fighting in the Assembly."

In September, the garrison learned that the Cherokee had betrayed a peace agreement that was to have allowed the prisoners they held hostage at Fort Loudoun safe passage back to South Carolina. "Relieving Fort Loudoun was Montgomery's intent last summer," Waddell told them. "But he fell short, although he ravaged many Cherokee villages on the way. This massacre of the Fort Loudoun commander and his men will be the Cherokee's revenge for Montgomery's attack, and now, there will be hell to pay for the Cherokees."

There *was* going to be hell to pay, and frustrated with his own state's inability to wage war against these savages, Will decided to find a way to join the efforts of South Carolina. The English had long since given up the "peace first" approach, as the Cherokees had continued to attack and slaughter white settlers throughout the region. With the French all but defeated on the western front, the aim of the English appeared to be the complete elimination of the tribes. A brutal retribution, but one Will understood might be the only solution to the continuing terror on the frontier.

He left Fort Dobbs to join Colonel Thomas Middleton's South Carolina provincial regiment. When he arrived at Fort Prince George in the upcountry of South Carolina, he joined almost three thousand men—British redcoats and colonial provincials—gathered under the command of Colonel James Grant, who Will later learned was a Highlander like himself. But unlike himself, intensely loyal to the British.

"Gentlemen," Grant addressed the forces the evening before they departed. He spoke from astride a handsome black horse. "General Amherst has charged me with punishing the Cherokee nation for all the damage they have inflicted upon our men, in particular those at Fort Loudoun whom they betrayed and massacred. But ours will not be an extensive campaign either. The terrain and difficulty of getting supplies further into the interior are against us, as Colonel Montgomery learned in last year's offensive.

"No, ours is to be a swift and punishing raid only to as far as the Middle Towns. We have learned that Colonel Byrd in Virginia plans to strike the Overhill towns in a similar manner. In this way, we should be able to eradicate the nation and these troubles once and for all."

Will noted there was no mention of any effort on the part of North Carolina to assist in these operations. He saw Grant signal to another officer who rode to his side on a beautiful chestnut stallion. "This is Lieutenant Francis Marion. He will be leading an advance guard into the pass where Montgomery found such difficulty."

"Bloody death march that'll be," he heard one of the soldiers who stood near him utter.

The following morning, the entire body of armed men headed out from Fort Prince George. Will rode alongside others from North Carolina who had come in service to the provincials to their south. He was ashamed of his own colony for not standing tall against this enemy as these men were doing.

Will had never seen the mountains which he'd heard so much about, and as he approached North Carolina from the south, he looked eagerly toward the horizon until he saw them rising in the distance, a deep blue silhouette against the summer sky. At first, he was slightly disappointed, thinking them lacking the grandeur he'd expected, but as the troops moved closer, the mountains gradually took on a different aspect—steep, densely forested, dark, and it seemed to Will, foreboding.

When they reached the deep gorge wherein Montgomery had taken such a beating, Marion and thirty of his men struck out ahead of the main army. Within a short time, Will and the others heard the gunshots, war whoops, and screams of the injured and dying, but after a time, one of Marion's men raced back to where the provincials and regular British troops waited, giving the signal for them to move. The provincials went in first, and taking the advice of Marion's man, they entered the gorge not in regular file, as was the British custom. Instead, they kept to the trees, dodging the accurate fire of the Cherokee. They were followed by the uniformed soldiers.

At the end of the fight, the Cherokee, low on ammunition, withdrew, and Grant's troops moved across the river and into the territory of the Middle Towns. Will had fought and likely killed some of the Indians, but he couldn't be sure. He rode with the troops into the first village they came to, Echoe, and he watched as Grant's men shot any remaining villagers and set fire to their miserable cabins that were not much more than hovels. He had no stomach for such things, although they'd been ordered by Grant, and so he stood to one side, observing. He became aware of someone at his side and turned to see Francis Marion, filthy and battle worn but a survivor of the death march, watching as well.

"This makes me sick," Marion said. "These poor creatures. We surely should not grudge them their miserable habitations."

Will watched in equal despair, and when he saw the ripe cornfields being cut down and knowing one of the main food sources for these people was being destroyed, he felt his devil had been dealt with. He wasn't a regular in the militia, only a volunteer from another state, and he had no desire to continue on Grant's planned destruction of other Middle Town villages. He had taken his revenge for what had been done to his family.

Oddly, it didn't feel all that good.

He turned his horse and headed east toward what remained of his family.

The sun was setting behind the tall forest trees when Will heard the music. A haunting tune, sounding almost mystical. Like someone playing a flute. He dismounted and grabbed his rifle. Cautiously, he crept through the underbrush, trying to be as quiet as possible. He smelled wood smoke and saw a glow of a campfire through the trees. Instinctively, he wanted to turn back, but then he saw a figure silhouetted against the firelight.

The figure of a woman. A woman with a gun. A white woman.

What the hell was a woman, a white woman, doing out here in the wilderness? His curiosity overcame his caution, and he stepped forward into the clearing. Seeing the fear in her eyes, slowly he dropped his rifle and raised his hands. "Don't shoot," he said.

"Who're you?" the woman uttered, taking aim at his heart.

"Name's Will. Will Gordon. I won't hurt you."

Chapter Seventeen

Fiona Cassidy, widow of a Cherokee brave killed the year before in battle with the British, had hidden away in the woods with her family when once again the British launched a deadly attack on their village. Facing the intruder, her heart pounded so heavily it sent blood rushing to her ears. "Then leave us," she demanded. She adjusted her stance and raised her head just enough to see him more clearly. He was a tall, lanky fellow with reddish brown hair and light blue eyes. He looked like someone she knew back in Ireland. "You Irish?" she asked.

"Scot," he replied. "A Highlander." And then he greeted her in Gaelic.

Fiona frowned but lowered her gun just a little. "How is it you came upon my camp?"

He grinned. "Heard the sound of a flute."

She swore silently to herself. She hadn't thought of the music giving them away. "So, what are you doing out here anyway? Are you a trader?"

"No. I'm just a farmer out of place," was his simple reply. Something about him diminished Fiona's fear. Maybe it was the Gaelic. Maybe it was his unthreatening manner. He'd not tried to pick up his weapon, nor did he try to approach her further. But he did return her question. "What are you doing out here all alone?"

"I'm not alone," she blurted without thinking. She didn't want him to believe she had no one looking out for her, but she may have betrayed the safety of her children and the others who were in hiding.

He looked around warily but apparently saw no one. "Who are you? This is no country for white women."

She raised her chin defiantly. "This is no country for farmers out of place either, sir. I ask again, why are you here?"

The man lowered his head and took a deep breath. "I rode with the South Carolina militia to invade the Cherokee lands."

Fiona's blood turned cold. "Did you bring them with you? Are we to become your next victims?" she challenged.

"I left them back at Echoe," he told her. "I can't abide what they are doing. I have no fondness for the Cherokee. Some of them killed my wife and some of my family. Neither do I have the appetite for the kind of murder and destruction the English and their colonists have in mind with these raids. I'm on my way back east, to my daughter and friends."

Fiona considered this a moment. Her Cherokee husband was dead, their village likely destroyed, and a part of her had longed to leave the Indians and return to her own kind. Perhaps this was a way out. "Do you know your way?"

"Just following the sun. It always comes up in the east."

"Aren't you afraid? There are still many Indians in these mountains who'd as soon kill you as look at you."

"What about you? You're white. Aren't you afraid of being killed?"

"More afraid of being killed by white men than Indians," she retorted. And then she spoke something in Cherokee, and Maura, holding Nanyeh's hand, emerged from the woods.

"This is my daughter. She is of my Cherokee husband who was killed last summer in the English raid. And my friend, Nanyeh, the child's grandmother."

The man stared at her in open disbelief. "How? Why?"

"'Tis too long of a story, and you are a stranger. I trust no one."

The man hesitated, then looked quizzically at Fiona. "Are you going back to one of those villages? Because I can tell you now, there will be nothing to go back to. Grant and his men are taking anything of value and burning everything else to the ground."

At this Nanyeh let out a small cry and turned her back to the fire. Fiona wanted to drop her gun and go to her, but she feared the intruder would then attack them. She spoke again in Cherokee in a loud voice, and moments later, a black woman and a young boy, and a second boy with flaming red hair came into the camp. "Take his gun," Fiona directed the woman whom she called Alicia.

To Will Gordon she said, "Don't you lay a hand on her."

The man didn't move as Alicia retrieved his gun and aimed it at him. No one spoke for a long moment, then Fiona felt her son tug at her skirt.

"Ma," he said in a small voice. "Is he my Da?"

Chapter Eighteen

Fiona sat up talking with Will Gordon long into the night and decided in the end that it would be better to accept his invitation to accompany him back to white civilization than to risk anything further in Indian country. It was partly what she'd wanted deep down in her heart, to return to her people, but another part of her was torn. The Cherokee had become her people too.

Mostly, she wanted to see her children to a safer place.

She found Will to be a quiet man who seemed to think things through before taking action. He'd apparently thought long and hard before joining the English soldiers in their raid on the Indians because he'd made it clear he hated the English. He had not yet told her why, but she sensed that he had suffered something terrible under the English at some time in his life. She was puzzled that a man who so hated the British would join them, but he seemed remorseful that he'd done so, and she decided in any case, her options were few: stay here and probably starve, die, or be captured or go with him back to white civilization in eastern North Carolina.

Another journey! Fiona recalled her mystical granny reading the tea leaves the night before she left Ireland, destined for Charlestown as an indentured servant. Destined for a horror she could never forget. "Journeys," her granny had foretold. "There's more coming to you than this ocean voyage..." The prediction had come true already, and now it seemed as if yet another journey lay ahead.

***

The small group of refugees, Fiona and her children Aidan and Maura, the elderly Cherokee woman Nanyeh, Alicia and her little brother Abe, and Will left the camp as the eastern sky lightened, although the sun remained behind the mountain peaks for some time. Nanyeh walked with them a short distance, then held back. "I must stay with my people," she said. "No matter this war between us and whites. I belong here, in Cherokee land. I am a war woman."

Fiona went to her and held the old woman tightly in her arms. Both shook in grief and unabashedly shed their tears. Then Fiona sniffed and said, "I understand, Nanyeh. I too now must go back to my own people. But you have been kind to me, taught me many things, shared your beloved son with me and helped raise our children. I am grateful, and I will always remember you."

Nanyeh pulled away slightly and said, "If you see Quella, tell her I will see her on the other side when we have both gone to the Great Spirit." And then she turned and disappeared into the thick forest.

Fiona stared after her a long while, her heart heavy, knowing that Nanyeh was going there to die. Realizing that Will stood watching from a distance, waiting, she turned to him. "She's not going with us."

"So I heard. I'm sorry for you. Another loss. But she is right. I don't know how she would be treated by those who hate the Indians."

"How do you think they will treat my daughter?" Fiona asked somberly.

He shook his head. "I honestly don't know. There have been Indians living among whites in our settlements. Some have married whites, but folks have mixed feelings about that."

Fiona looked back to where Nanyeh had walked into the forest, and for a moment strongly considered following her. But if she did, she might risk not only her own life, but those of her children, and Alicia and her brother. If they weren't killed, but caught, she might be sent back to the plantation and her rapist, and Alicia and Abe, runaway slaves, were likely to be hanged. She turned back to Will.

"Let's go."

***

They made their way east along riverbanks and over mountains. They had a single horse among them, the one Will rode on the military march, and he let Maura and Aidan take turns riding when their little legs grew tired. Their meager belongings, including Fiona's old woolen satchel, were tied in bundles on the horse as well. They followed the waterways as much as possible, but kept to the shadows of the forests, hoping to remain out of sight of any hostile Indians that might be nearby. When they made camp, they kept the fire low and put it out as soon as they had no more need for it.

The first night out, Aidan and Will went to a stream near their camp and returned with a fat trout. "I showed him our way to fish," Aidan said proudly, presenting his mother with their dinner.

Fiona smiled but was troubled when she realized that her son considered himself Indian.

Our way to fish... She recalled how her husband Onacona, called White Owl, had taken him to the woods even as a small boy and taught him the Indian ways of hunting and fishing, how to track a deer, how to shoot a blowgun and his small bow and arrow. Yes, he was part Indian, she figured, despite having white skin and red hair. He even called himself by his Cherokee name, Firehead. How would he fit into the white man's world, a place he'd never known?

Later that night, after they had settled into their blankets, Fiona arose and went to where Will was on guard, sitting up against a tree trunk. "Thank you for taking us with you," she said quietly. "I know we must be a burden."

"It's better than riding alone," he replied, shifting his position and rubbing one of his toes. "I'm glad of the company."

"Is something wrong with your toe?"

He gave a small laugh. "Old injury. It's nothing." Then he told her of how it was broken on his sixteenth birthday: "There's this old Scottish tradition, a trial to test a fellow's readiness for manhood. The *clach cuid fir*, the lifting stone," he explained. "To prove you have become a man, you must raise up a boulder." His grin was almost sheepish as he told her how his toe was injured.

"You dropped the stone on your foot," Fiona stated with undisguised amusement. Men!

Will nodded and continued. "It hurt like fire. A woman from the village tried to set it for me, and I got an early taste of whisky that day. Later, I found I couldn't work in the field with the splint on, so I took it off before I should have, and the toe's never been the same since." He shrugged. "I'm not lame, though. It just flares up from time to time."

"Does it hurt now?" she asked, but without waiting for a reply, Fiona went to her satchel and brought him a piece of willow bark. "Here. Chew on this. In a few minutes, you should feel some relief."

He looked at her suspiciously, as if she were offering him poison, then accepted the chip of bark and slowly began chewing. They sat in silence, staring at the remaining embers of the fire. The night was cool, but it was mountain summertime cool, refreshing rather than chilling.

At length Will said, "This is helping. Thank you. What is it?"

"White willow bark. It's what the Indians use for pain. I learned about it from Nanyeh and Quella."

"Quella," Will said, looking up sharply. "I heard Nanyeh speak of saying farewell to someone named Quella. Who is that?"

Fiona looked at him in surprise. "Her sister. Also, my friend. She is a medicine woman, and to whites up in the northern mountains, she's served as a healer and midwife. Why do you ask?" She saw a strange expression on his face, a mixture of astonishment and disbelief.

"It was many years ago," he said. "My wife, Margaret, was about to give birth to our daughter, Jeannette. It was a cold January night, and there was no one to help us. And then this woman just appeared out of nowhere. Her name was Quella. She brought our daughter safely into this world, and then she just disappeared again."

Fiona was startled to hear this, but then considering Quella's penchant for wandering, and her mystical abilities that seemed to connect her to those who needed her, she wasn't totally surprised. "I doubt there are many medicine women in these mountains named Quella," she replied. "And the Quella I know comes and goes in mysterious ways. It most likely was her."

Fiona paused, then added, "I learned much from her and her sister, Nanyeh. I hope one day I become a medicine woman myself."

Why she admitted that to Will, a near perfect stranger, she had no idea. She had thought about it, even discussed it with Nanyeh, who had encouraged her and taught her many secrets of Indian healing. But it was Quella who, in addition to her knowledge of healing plants and mystical spells, had had the strongest spirit vision, the Sight. It was her ability to know of things before they happened, and how she knew to show up when she was needed that set her apart and even above Nanyeh as a medicine woman.

Only at this moment did Fiona realize that Quella's powerful Sight was the difference between an adept medicine woman and an almost magical healer. Her Granny had told her she had the Sight if she would only work to strengthen it. Could she become as powerful a healer as Quella? She reached into her pocket and drew out the talisman stone, given to her by her Granny many years ago, the night she left Ireland. Silently she traced the Gaelic circles with her finger and felt a power emanate from it that she'd not known before. The power that was to be hers. Now she knew why Granny had given it to her. Not for luck, or protection, but to confirm her destiny when she at last comprehended it.

Chapter Nineteen

They traveled for days with no sign of Indians or outlaws, who Will had told her also posed a serious threat to settlers. "They've been known to ride into settlements and farms and raise false alarms about encroaching Indian raiders, then when the settlers fort up in whatever stockades are near enough to offer safety, they steal everything, and blame it on the Indians."

Each day, Aidan asked to start their journey walking alongside Will. The boy with the fiery red hair didn't talk a lot, but he seemed to take comfort in the presence of a man. Fiona wondered if he thought Will Gordon was his real father, even though they'd both told him that wasn't the case. But in her heart, she knew it was a father, a real father, he longed for.

They traveled for as many hours each day as they could, passing the time by sharing their stories. Fiona was surprised at how easily she found it to talk to Will Gordon. He seemed to open up easily to her as well, as if they'd known one another a long time, although both had difficulty relating the horrors that had eventually led to their meeting on a lonely mountaintop in North Carolina. For the most part, they spoke only when the children were out of earshot.

His story broke her heart. He'd been but a boy of twelve when he and all his kinsmen were called by their feudal landlord, Lord Lewis Gordon, to fight the British at a battle on Culloden Moor, in the Scottish Highlands, where they all died except him. "By some miracle, I awoke in the dark and managed to run away from that killing field."

He told her how he immigrated to Wilmington and traveled up the Cape Fear River to Cross Creek and a settlement of Scottish Highlanders, where he'd married Margaret McKinney, daughter of the man who'd brought a group of other immigrants from the Isle of Skye. "I loved that man like a Da," Will said, choking when he spoke. "And I loved his daughter."

She was horrified to learn that after the family had moved from

Cross Creek into the Yadkin River Valley, Margaret and her parents were murdered by Indians in revenge for real or imagined injustices done to them by the white man. "I was warned by a trader, a man named Greenlee, that it was dangerous to remain in the area, but I didn't heed..." At this point, Will stopped, unable to continue.

"Don't say more," Fiona said softly, touching his arm. But she now clearly understood why this seemingly kind, gentle man had joined forces with the brutal British, whom he hated: to take revenge for his family's murder. An eye for an eye. Not that different from Dragging Canoe's killing of twenty-three whites to pay for the killing of twenty-three Indians.

"Did making the assault on Echoe heal your grief?" she asked him bluntly, even somewhat accusingly.

He didn't answer right away, but then replied, "No. But it did make me realize that killing innocents to punish the guilty makes no sense, no matter which side you are on."

Will was silent for a long while, then he stopped walking suddenly and scratched his chin. "I hadn't thought about Greenlee in a long time," he mused. "I recall now it was him who was at our cabin when Margaret was pregnant. He told us about a midwife he knew up in the mountains, kind of a granny woman, and said if he came across her, he'd tell her about our baby. Then the night Jeannette was born, Quella showed up. Do you suppose...?"

Fiona smiled. "Probably so," was all she said.

It took courage, but Fiona finally decided to trust Will with her own difficult story, and as they walked, he learned how she'd arrived in America only to be brutally abused by Nigel Stainton, and how she'd escaped to the mountains to live with the Indians. "Aiden does not know who his real father was, nor do I want him to ever find out," she said to Will. "Promise me you will keep this secret forever."

***

Eventually they crossed a wide river at its confluence with a smaller tributary that led directly east, which narrowed as they followed it into a long valley with rich lands that beckoned cultivation. "I heard about this place, if we're where I think we are," Will told her. "A friend of mine,

Sam Davidson, said there's a lot of frontiersmen who are itching to get to this land, but by treaty, being west of the mountain range, it's still Cherokee country."

They camped that night at the river's edge, and as they had encountered no hostiles of any sort, Fiona dared to take out her flute as they sat by the fire. She decided to try to play her favorite fiddle tune, Grey Eagle, as best as she could with the flute. It wasn't a rousing success, but she caught the general gist of the tune, and when she finished, she saw Will staring at her.

"Where'd you learn that?" he asked.

"From my Da," she said. "It's a fiddle tune, not made for this," she indicated the flute.

"Fergus played it on the fiddle," he said. "Sounds quite different from the flute. Play it again."

Unsure if this was a criticism or compliment, she tried it again, and again it fell short of what she would have liked, but no fiddle being at hand, it would do. Aidan, Maura, Alicia and Abe got into the spirit of the moment and began to dance around the fire ring, creating a frolic that left them all laughing at the end. Fiona realized how long it had been since they had laughed and decided it didn't matter if the tune didn't sound much like the fiddle version.

"I think we should call this place Grey Eagle," she told them when the music stopped.

Taking out his knife, Will carved the initials "G.E." into a nearby sycamore tree at the edge of the river. "And so it is. Grey Eagle."

The following morning, the river wound off to the north, but the small group left it behind and headed steadily eastward as the sun rose. Will guided them over a high mountain pass where they connected with yet another river. "I believe we are at the headwaters of the Catawba River," he said. "My friend Sam has been out here with his brothers, scouting. I think that family plans to settle around here somewhere, once this Indian business is behind us."

Fiona wasn't sure how this "Indian business" would end, but she saw no reconciliation between the two cultures, at least not anytime soon. "Aren't we still in Cherokee territory?"

"Not by treaty, but they still use this as hunting grounds. Catawbas hunt here as well."

The thought of coming across a hunting party of either tribe gave Fiona a chill. "How do you know so much about this place? Are we nearing Corbinton?"

Will laughed. "Hardly. We've many a mile to go before we reach there. But we are gaining on territory that's been settled by whites. I only know this place by hearsay. Sam's a big storyteller. Some of his favorite tales are about a man named Hunting John McDowell and my former neighbor, Daniel Boone. They're both true backwoodsmen, hunters and trappers who have crossed the mountains and hunted on forbidden land for years."

Fiona thought she'd heard of this Daniel Boone from stories told around Cherokee campfires. It seemed he got around and was friends with both white and red. Like Quella. And herself. It was possible, but not easy. She looked at Aidan and Maura, who were walking ahead of them. Aidan white, Maura red. They were holding hands.

***

The high mountains softened into rolling hills as they continued their eastward journey, keeping the blue ridges of the mountains to their left and walking along a path beside the river. It was late afternoon when suddenly Fiona thought she heard someone speak, and she stopped to listen. The wind whispered in the treetops, and the water trickled over ancient stones, but there was no one other than their small party anywhere nearby, so she continued on.

"Fiona." She heard it again. Someone, or something, was calling her name.

"Will, can we stop here for a rest?" she called out to him. They led the horse to the river's edge for a drink, and the children jumped into the cooling, refreshing water.

"What is it?" Will asked her, taking a seat on a rock next to her. "Are you alright?"

"I...I guess it's nothing," she replied, unsure of whether she'd heard anything at all. "I just fancied that I heard someone calling my name." That, she figured, would probably give Will Gordon pause at having taken her along on this journey. He must think her mad.

He didn't speak but reached over and took her hand in his. "We've a way to go yet, and we've been pushing hard. We'll slow our pace if you need it."

The touch of his hand sent a shiver through her, a sensation she hadn't felt before, not even with Onacona. It was a primal longing, as if she had found a part of her that had been missing. Startled and frightened, she pulled her hand away and stood up. "I'm fine. I'm sure it was just the wind I heard." She called to the children to come out of the river and dry off so they could be on their way. As they started out again, she found she was trembling, and she was unsure whether it was from hearing her name on the wind or the touch of Will Gordon's hand.

They continued along the riverside path until they came upon a break in the forest that opened onto a broad meadow with golden grass swaying gently in a warm afternoon breeze.

"Fiona," she heard again. This time she was certain of it, and she stopped again and turned her face to the sun. An image sprang into her mind, a clear vision of a homestead here in this meadow. Her home. Blinking, she shook her head and the image quickly vanished, but her spirit vision, her own power of Sight, told her she would one day return here. It was this land calling to her.

CHAPTER TWENTY

After the incident in the valley of the golden grasses, as she had begun to call the place in her vision, and even more after the unsettling sensations stirred by Will's touch, Fiona was troubled. What did these signs mean? Were they portents of the future, or figments of her imagination? Was she truly going mad? But the closer they got to the white settlements, the more at ease Fiona became. Will had not approached her again, at least not in any way that might be construed as an overture, nor had she heard any more phantom voices.

Hers was an uncertain future, to be sure, this new life among white settlers, but nothing could be worse than some of the things she'd left behind. She kept this in mind, and the talisman stone in her hand, as she walked.

* * *

Days later they arrived at Fort Dobbs, where Will reported his action to Colonel Waddell, under whom he'd served as part of a local militia. He'd told Fiona he wasn't sure if he would be considered a deserter for leaving the North Carolina company to join Grant and his South Carolina raiders, but Waddell seemed to care less about that than trying to re-recruit Will to join the regiment he'd been ordered to gather to fight with Colonel Byrd in Virginia .

"With all respect, sir," Will said to his former commander and comrade in arms, "I'm done with fighting for now. I've made my peace with the deaths of my family, and now I'm escorting these women and children to Corbinton and hopefully to a safer place than the frontier."

Will remained confounded by the woman he'd encountered on this journey. Fiona Cassidy had suffered greatly, mostly at the hands of the English. And yet, her resilience and courage amazed him. He wasn't sure what to do with her. Or about her. He wasn't sure, in fact, what he would do himself when he arrived at Corbinton with a red-headed Irish woman, her son and half-breed daughter, and two runaway slaves. But he knew he'd been right to encourage them to leave Cherokee country.

It was likely to become a bloodbath soon, if not already.

He bartered with one of the incoming recruits for a second horse, and after resting near the fort for three days, he and Fiona and the others resumed their eastward trek. Will didn't mean to make a detour, but without thinking of where he was going, he found himself off course and heading directly back to the farm where the massacre of his family had taken place. When after a couple of hours on the road he realized what he had done, and he brought them to a halt under a large sycamore tree.

"What is it, Will?" Fiona asked.

Will's chest tightened suddenly, and he struggled to breathe. He didn't answer her straightaway. Then he replied, "I've taken us off our path."

"Are we lost?" Aidan wanted to know.

Will gave him a sad smile. "No, son, we're not lost." But he wondered if indeed he was still lost in his sorrow and grief. Could he bear to go back to their homestead? He could change course now and head toward Salisbury without losing too much time. But something was pulling at him, and he knew he had to return to the home he'd known with Margaret, to say a final farewell to her and her parents at their graves. He'd satisfied his need for revenge in Indian country, but he had still to put to rest the memory of what had happened. He was curious, too, to know who, if anyone, had taken ownership of the cabins they had built.

"Fiona," he said, looking not at her but in the direction of his old home. "There's something I need to do before we continue to Corbinton. Someplace I need to go."

"'Tis your old home, isn't it?" she replied, following his gaze. He found it uncanny, her seeming ability to read his thoughts. It had happened more than once along the way.

"Aye."

"Do you want us to go with you? Or should we go back to the fort and wait for you?"

He turned and looked into her hazel eyes flecked with gold, and he saw deep compassion in her expression. "'Tis something I need to do alone," he told her.

She nodded, and nothing else was spoken between them. They simply turned around and went back to the safety of the fort, where they would wait for Will to return.

Will was grateful for her understanding. She was still much of a mystery to him, and her ways were curious, part Irish, part Indian. But she had proven her mettle on the long journey through rugged mountains and thick forests, and he held a deep respect for her. He was sorry for her many losses as well, and especially for the brutal treatment she'd received from the man who'd raped her.

It was late in the day when he came upon the deserted shell of the cabin he'd once called home. The structure was still standing, but weeds clogged the yard, and vines had overtaken the houses. He tethered his horse, took gun in hand, and stepped up onto his porch, which sagged slightly beneath his weight. It had been more than two years since that horrid day, and it seemed to him as if the cabin had grieved its loss too.

He pushed his way through a mass of spider webs and stepped inside. He was surprised to find that their belongings had not been totally looted by the marauding murderers or anyone else, it appeared. The bedding had been shredded, Margaret's rifle was missing from its rack, and their stores of cornmeal were strewn about, moldering on the wooden table and dirt floor. But pots and pans and other cooking utensils hung just as they were the day of the attack.

He found the same to be true of the cabin Fergus, Esther, and Mary had occupied. The shed that had protected their livestock had fallen down, as had the henhouse where his sister-in-law, Mary, always afraid of everything, had met with a skunk. Despite his sadness, Will had to give a small laugh at that memory. The smithy was still there but was sagging to one side.

And then he looked beyond the homestead, up the incline to where he and his friends, George Paterson and Gil Murrey, had hastily buried them. They'd had no time to create grave markers that day. Could he find where he'd laid them to rest?

But their graves were easy to spot, where the earth had sunk below the surface of the surrounding hillside. He knelt beside the one he knew was Margaret's and ran his hands across the weeds that now covered it over. "I am so sorry, my darling," he murmured. "I am so sorry." And for a long while, grief and guilt stole over him once again, and he wept.

At last, he stood and returned to search through the remains of the smithy, where he found his blacksmithing tools and others, including a hammer, saw, and shovel. He cut some boards from the side of the building and created three rough-hewn crosses which he placed at the heads of the three graves. The late summer sun was descending in a show of brilliant gold, as if to honor the memories of these he'd loved so dearly.

He returned to the cabin and found a blanket that had not been slashed by the Indians. In it he bundled the most needed tools from the smithy and tied it to his horse. He was about to leave the cabin when a ray of the setting sun glinted on something lodged at the edge of the loft.

It was the fiddle and bow Fergus had given him on his sixteenth birthday. He reached for it and stroked it gently, remembering the many good times he'd had playing it with Fergus while Margaret and others danced into the night. It was as if he'd been given a gift all over again, one of forgiveness and hope for a brighter tomorrow.

He found the other fiddle in Fergus's cabin, and taking it and a few mementos that he would someday give to Jeannette, he left the homestead and returned to Fort Dobbs. He couldn't bring Margaret back to life, but at her grave, he'd promised to make a good life for Jeannette.

Maybe she'd learn to play the fiddle like her grandpa.

Then he remembered Fiona saying that Grey Eagle was a fiddle tune. Did she play the fiddle as well?

CHAPTER TWENTY-ONE

Hillsborough (formerly Corbinton), North Carolina, Autumn 1767

Fiona Cassidy Gordon stood in the doorway of her small log home and watched Jeannette and Maura harvesting late summer vegetables from their kitchen garden. Aidan and Abe were working with Will in the nearby field. Inside, little Fergus, now almost three, napped in the small bed Will had fashioned for him.

Six years had passed since she'd left Cherokee country. She and Will had been married now for almost five, and she'd worked as hard at becoming part of the society of the settlement community as she had to integrate with the Cherokee in Echoe.

It had been an odd experience for her, as Maura was clearly half Indian, and folks didn't know what to make of a white woman who'd been married to an Indian. She knew that many whispered behind her back that she must have been "taken" by an Indian, not married to one. No one except Will ever knew of Aidan's origin or she might have been ostracized even more, women always being blamed for such incidents when the perpetrator was white.

Will and Fiona had portrayed Alicia and Abe as being their property, not about to reveal they were runaway slaves. They'd offered to take legal action to attain their freedom, but Alicia wanted no part of that. "I'd rather us stay on with you," she'd said to Fiona, almost in tears. "We been together since before Abe was born. I don't know no other life, and if we don't belong to someone, we might just get snatched away again by somebody else as their slaves." Knowing that had happened to others who had become freemen, Will and Fiona at last agreed to the arrangement, at least on the surface.

Their home was outside of town on George Paterson's farm, where Will, Aidan, and Abe helped work the land and run the grist mill. Will had set up a smithy not far from their cabin and was teaching Aidan the craft of blacksmithing. The Paterson family, including Will's former sister-in-law Mary, had never once questioned Fiona about her past. Instead, they had lovingly included her and her children in their family of friends. It might have been due to their earlier history with Will, but Fiona never felt any undercurrent that she was not welcomed.

When they'd first arrived in Hillsborough, which until last year had been called Corbinton, they had visited the local mercantile store, and she was astounded to find Captain John Michael, the former ship's captain, now at the helm of a prosperous business. When she saw him, she rushed to him with a hearty embrace without thinking about the looks she was given by other customers.

"Captain Michael!" she cried. "What are you doing here?"

The merchant just laughed, but he was obviously surprised and delighted to see her again.

"Not a captain anymore," he replied with a laugh. "I said I never wanted to take another cargo such as we had on board the *Lady Caroline*, and when the owner demanded me to do so again, I left him and returned to America. It was you," he added with a nod toward the well-supplied store, "that gave me the notion that I could be a trader, or as in this case, a merchant."

"Is Danny with you?" she wanted to know, looking around in case her former kitchen assistant had decided to follow his captain to a different life. But she felt the answer before he even replied, and her throat tightened when he spoke.

"No," the former captain said, and his expression turned sad. "He was lost at sea shortly after we left you at Charlestown. Went aloft when he shouldn't have, trying to prove his mettle I guess, and fell."

"I...I'm very sorry to hear that. He was a good lad."

"Aye, that he was." John Michael paused, as if remembering something. "Wait here a moment," he said and walked briskly to the rear of the store, disappearing behind a curtain.

When he returned, he held a familiar object in his hand. Mr. Bentley's Irish flute. "I found it in Danny's hammock after he died," he explained. "Nobody else seemed to want it, and I was, after all, the ship's captain, so I brought it along when I came ashore for good." He eyed it. "Doesn't do me any good, since I can't play it. But I recall you were quite accomplished with it." He smiled and handed it to Fiona. "I think Danny would like you to have it."

* * *

Life was easier here than in either Charlestown or Echoe, but times were difficult nonetheless. Years of drought had hurt the local farmers, and money was scarce. John Michael had extended credit to many of them as far as he could, but his business was threatened by their inability to pay. The only physician available was an itinerant doctor who visited the community at unpredictable intervals. Once the townspeople learned of Fiona's skills with herbal medicine and midwifery, she was often called upon to attend to the sick, wounded, and childbearing mothers. Rarely was she paid, but often she would find a loaf of bread or a basket of eggs at her doorstep from a family she had served. They were a proud lot overall and didn't want to be beholden to anyone.

Fiona had watched the town change dramatically in the short time she'd been here. Some wealthy, well-educated northerners had moved here, infiltrating the political system and bringing much corruption to the local government. She found these newcomers rather odious. They reminded her of the men who'd gathered in Nigel Stainton's home that fateful day when she and Beatrice had served the meal that ended up causing her such grief.

Rich. Powerful. Arrogant.

And likely dangerous. All loyal to the English king and his representative in the North Carolina colony, Governor Tryon.

It was common knowledge that sheriffs were appointed by the Crown from among the freeholders according to who paid the most to obtain the job. Once in office, they made up for it by charging exorbitant fees and fines for made up charges and undocumented tax payments and pocketed at least half of the money.

It was only the tip of the wave of corruption that was sweeping across North Carolina, and Fiona knew that Will and others were angry and frustrated at this renewed English supremacy in a land that was supposed to be freer and less restricted.

Knowing how to read and write, Fiona schooled her children and those of her neighbors. Aidan had tolerated his lessons, but it was obvious to Fiona he didn't care much for that type of learning. Instead, his love was for the open air and deep forests. They were his true classrooms.

"I'm not needing school anymore," he told her one day, and she didn't insist he continue. He had a fair knowledge of language by now, and could read, although his spelling was atrocious.

Aidan wandered into the woods often, sometimes being gone for more than a day, which made the family anxious, but when he returned, he usually brought a prize in the form of a deer or turkey. He seemed a natural born woodsman, and Fiona tried not to worry. He was fourteen now and growing into a strong, sturdy young man, and she was grateful he'd learned such skills from Onacona. Hillsborough wasn't the frontier, but the frontier lay not far away, and it wouldn't surprise her any if Aidan Cassidy, her little Firehead, returned there one day.

***

"I've had enough," Will said one night as he returned from the field. He told Fiona that George Paterson's grist mill had come under notice of seizure by the government for nonpayment of taxes. "They won't accept my corn or services in barter for the taxes," George had told Will. "There is no money around here, as you well know. How do they expect us to pay them? Barter is all we have, and what we all use these days."

Will continued, "There's talk about organizing settlers like us to try to get better government around here. I heard Hermon Husband is holding a meeting this evening, and I think I will go."

Fiona knew about this as well. They called themselves the Regulators. They were mostly frontiersmen who'd arrived long before these officials, a loosely organized group who were protesting the corrupt practices of the newcomers who'd quickly used their money and knowledge of the law to take control. The settlers were used to greater freedom and relatively fair treatment, not this English-style heavy handed government. Many of them had immigrated to America precisely to leave just such treatment.

"I will go with you," she said firmly, even though women generally did not attend such meetings. Will only nodded, and Fiona saw a slight smile cross his face.

***

Although Hermon Husband claimed he was not one of the Regulators, Will found him to be an effective instigator of discontent among those gathered at the meeting. His words spoke the truth of what was happening to the backcountry people. "There is no regulation of legal fees and tax levies, and consequently, Edmund Fanning and other county officials have been robbing our pockets to line theirs," he told the assembly, which was followed by a chorus of huzzahs. "We have no say in matters of government. I say we petition the officials to hear our grievances in a court of law."

No chance, Will thought. It was those very officials who were corrupt. Why would they want to hear anything that would threaten their lucrative practices, and their power? As they left the meeting, George remarked, "Husband isn't a violent man, but a lot of the rest of this lot are not above taking the law in their own hands. I'd be careful if I was Fanning or one of those other officials."

Will looked at his friend askance. "What? Fight the English? With what? Our hoes and pitchforks?"

George grinned sheepishly and shrugged. "I know. It's not practical, but there are times I wouldn't mind giving that Fanning a good thrashing. He sets the bar for the others. He cheats. They cheat. And the governor looks the other way."

* * *

Will tried to avoid the increasing conflict between the backcountry men and the officials who ran the county. He knew first-hand what happened when one defied the British. First from Culloden, and again from Grant's ruthless destruction of Indian civilians. "They're merciless when they want something," Will told Fiona. "At least some here are level-headed enough to try to get the Assembly to hear them out and not take to arms."

A few days later, they learned that Governor Tryon was arriving in Hillsborough with a military force he'd managed to gather in other counties, and word spread quickly through the community, a rallying cry to meet him face-to-face. Will, George, Jake, Joe, and Aidan, who was now fifteen and considered himself a man, left the women to take care of the children and walked into town where they found a throng of protesters, mostly farmers and small merchants, gathered to submit a petition to the governor.

But when Tryon's well-armed force arrived, the governor was not with them. Instead, an officer read a proclamation, proposing to pardon all insurgents provided they give bond to pay their taxes, to abstain from further obstruction of the county officers, and take an oath of loyalty and allegiance to the king.

"That I will not do," Will uttered, fists clenched and face white as he turned and left.

CHAPTER TWENTY-TWO

Hillsborough, North Carolina, September 1770

For two more years, the struggle went on, with the small farmers and merchants pitted against a government giving only lukewarm attention to their complaints. Colonel Edmund Fanning, the registrar from Orange County and one accused of the crimes, was tried and found guilty of overcharging his fees, only to be fined a single penny as punishment.

One morning in late September news came that Justice Richard Henderson was convening the superior court in Hillsborough, an event which only happened twice a year, and would finally hear their case that very day.

But when Will, Fiona, and Aidan arrived at the courthouse, they found the judge had postponed the hearing until Monday, two days hence. The crowd that had gathered, already angry, booed and raised fists. Fiona wondered if the judge had hoped they would cool off before the hearing. They returned on Monday; however, the crowd had not cooled off. If anything, their anger seemed more heated.

When some of the Regulators stormed the courthouse, Will took Fiona firmly by the elbow. "Let's leave. This is turning ugly." But Aidan refused to leave.

When he returned home sometime later, Fiona learned that indeed, the day had turned out badly, at least for the officials. According to Aidan, the Regulators had gotten out of hand, had beaten one lawyer, then went after Fanning, who ran for his life once he escaped them.

Henderson had promised to hear their case, but turned tail and ran off, effectively closing the court, but Aidan gleefully related that the Regulators had taken over the court and tried the cases themselves.

Aidan was obviously thrilled at this outcome, but Fiona was troubled. "Sounds like to me it was a mob out of hand," she said. "I don't like what the government is doing in overlooking legitimate grievances, but I like less that those who hold those grievances have taken such illegal and dangerous steps to get their way."

"It was wrong what the English did to our Cherokee village, Ma," Aidan blurted out. "Onacona had no choice but to stand up to them. And they killed him!"

His words reopened old wounds that still ached at times, and she shot back, "And what good did it do? They just came back and will keep on coming until his people are destroyed."

Aidan jerked his chair back in a fit of fury. "Well, what should we do, just sit around and wait until they tax us to death and take our land like they took the Cherokees'? I would like to have been there when they thrashed Fanning. I heard his eye was almost beat out of his face."

"And I heard he's run away," Jeannette spoke up. "Good riddance, the coward."

Fiona was amazed at the vehemence in her children's words and attitude. She hadn't realized how closely they'd followed the events of the times, or the Regulators.

Will interrupted, trying to diffuse the situation. "I heard a wise woman say once," he looked over at Fiona, "that there are times to fight, and there are times to retreat. It doesn't make you a coward if you back off in a situation you can't win. The Cherokee know this, Jeannette. My guess is we'll see Fanning again. He indeed may be a coward, but he knows the governor will back him."

The room grew silent then. Maura and little Fergus were watching the older children and their parents with alarm. Suddenly, Aidan said, "I want to leave here."

Fiona's heart dropped. "But why? Where would you go?"

"Away from all this," he retorted. "Go somewhere I can be alone. Maybe become a long hunter. Or a trader, like McNeill. Somewhere there are no English. I hate the English. They are liars. They lied to Onacona's people, who are...or were...my people, about treaties. They've lied to all of us here about taxes. And they've cheated both sides as well."

Fiona was surprised he remembered McNeill. Aidan had been but a young boy when they'd left Echoe the second time, and McNeill and

Ma-ri had left the village the year before, moving into Virginia.

But before she could think of a reply, Will spoke, "It would be hard for you to go anywhere around here where there are no English. Maybe over the mountains, back into Cherokee lands, but the English, they're going to hunt all the Indians down. You won't escape anything, son."

But Aidan didn't want to hear it, and he turned his anger and frustration toward Will, a man who had taken him in and treated him like his own.

"Don't call me son," Aidan bit out. "My Da was Onacona. He is dead. I have no Da." And with that he slammed past the front door and out into the night.

Will started to follow him, but Fiona took his arm. "Let him go," she said quietly. "As you said, he is a man now, and he must sort things out for himself." She saw the hurt on Will's face, and she would like to have thrashed her son for his ungrateful behavior. She was surprised as well, since Will had been nothing but kind to Aidan, had in fact legally adopted him, and he had seemed to love Will in return.

Fiona suddenly physically felt her son's torment, and her whole body shuddered. She knew then that this anger and confusion had lain dormant in her son's soul since losing Onacona, her beloved White Owl.

White Owl had been his father, had been the one who raised him early on and who'd taught him to be an Indian. Will had become another father, teaching him the white man's ways. Her son was torn, it was clear, and only giving him his freedom to sort things out on his own would resolve his despair.

Jeannette began to cry, which led to Maura and Fergus setting up a wail. It was all Fiona could do not to cry herself. But as hard as it was to let him go, she knew it must be, at least for now.

By morning's light, Aidan Cassidy Gordon, her Firehead, was gone. Fiona and Will went to the smithy, which Aidan had taken as his own quarters when he reached his teen years and needed more privacy than he had in their small cabin. They found his bedroll, gun, and a couple of traps he'd forged himself were gone. Checking the barn, Aidan's horse was missing as well.

Fiona saw a slip of paper tacked to the wooden door. It read:

Dear Ma and Pa Will, I am Sory for my Rudness last Nit, but I must tak my Leev, at Leest for Now. Dont look for me. I will be Fin. A.

**The story continues in Book Three:
Fighting for Tomorrow**

Preview
Chapter One

Along the Watauga River, North Carolina, February 1771

The day was bleak, gray, and cold with a wet snow starting to fall as Aidan Cassidy Gordon made his way through the forest, looking for a likely place to camp along the river. He'd been on his solitary journey for several months now since leaving Hillsborough, and he was feeling his loneliness. Back at home, he'd heard the tales of the "long hunters," the rough frontiersmen who'd returned from a year or longer in the wilderness on their hunting expeditions and found them compelling. It had been his intent to become one of them, and maybe he still would, but this night, he wished he had more of a companion than his horse. He wasn't sure, but he thought it might be his birthday.

At first, his newfound freedom was exhilarating. He'd left in early fall and enjoyed the warm days and crisp nights and the blazing colors of the trees turning a thousand different shades of red, yellow, and orange. And then the leaves fell, and the trees lay barren and gray, sticks in the air, fallen leaves slick on the forest floor. The air turned from crisp to cool and then to cold. The winds in the high mountains were fierce, biting the flesh and letting the cold seep deep inside.

He'd managed to shoot the deer he needed for survival, and he'd cleaned as many hides as he could carry on the back of his horse in hopes of trading them for future supplies. He'd come across some isolated farms along his way, but nothing that resembled a village or settlement. People had told him about a place called Watauga, and he was headed there now, or at least he hoped so. The Indian part of him didn't want to admit it, but he was a little lost.

He'd heard that the Wataugans were settlers from Virginia and parts of North Carolina who'd grown both weary and wary of English rule, who'd defied the British treaty with the Indians and crossed over into Cherokee territory and settled there. Their settlement was somewhere along this river. When he found them, he hoped he could trade his deer hides to replenish his ammunition, buy a new gun, and resupply for his next foray into the wilderness.

A thin trail of smoke rising just beyond the next ridge caught his eye, and he took his well-used rifle in hand. He'd learned you could never be sure if people you encountered in this wilderness would be friend or foe. He'd met up with a few of both, Cherokees who attacked him for hunting on their lands, and a white trader who stole the first few of his deer hides after pretending to be friendly, even sharing Cass's evening meal before making off with his pelts.

The Cherokees he'd handled by speaking their language and identifying himself as being from Echoe.

Identifying himself. That was the problem.

He'd left home and come on this journey partly to try and find himself. Who was he? Was he white? Cherokee? Irish? English? His mother refused to speak of his blood father, other than to say that he was dead. She'd never told Cass who the man was, or how she came to be his wife, or even where they'd lived, except to say it was in South Carolina. Her real story remained a mystery to him—he knew there was much she hadn't told him, maybe never would.

He'd grown up knowing Indian ways, and the Cherokee ways of living off the land had served him well these past few months. Even now, when he looked up at the stars, he felt closer than ever to the man who had raised him from a tiny baby until the day an English bullet had taken his life. And then there was Will Gordon, who spoke English but with a strong accent, which he had been told was the dialect of the Highlanders of Scotland. Will had been kind to him and tried to be like a father, but he'd found it hard in his mind and his heart to replace his Cherokee father with a white man.

And yet his own skin was white, his hair red, much like Will's only brighter in color. His life in the white man's world had been tolerable, but only just. His mother had tried to school him in reading and writing, but he'd much preferred the education to be had from nature in the woodlands near their home. He cared not a fig for farming, but he did learn some blacksmithing skills from Will. Somehow, though, he just didn't fit there.

And then there was the thing about his name. His mother had named him Aidan, after her own father, but it wasn't a name he much liked. He had been called Firehead by Onacona and the others in the village. In Cherokee ways, women kept their own clan names even after marriage, and Fiona had kept the name of her Irish Cassidy family and gave it to him. But when she married Will Gordon, and he legally adopted her children, he became Aidan Cassidy Gordon. It all seemed overmuch to him. As he pondered these things during the months he'd been in the wilderness, he'd decided to follow the Cherokee tradition of changing one's name when the situation warranted and landed on Cass as a name sufficient for his needs.

He made his way up over the ridge, and looking down into the valley below, he saw a small cabin in a clearing from whence the smoke arose. It was almost dark, and he'd found no suitable camping spot, so he decided to risk it and see if he might take shelter here. A wagon stood beneath a large tree near the house, a horse tethered to the tree, covered with a blanket. This was not the dwelling of an Indian. Maybe he was getting close to the Wataugans.

Cass's horse whinnied when they approached the cabin, announcing their arrival, and a man with a grizzled beard opened the door, the barrel of his shotgun emerging before his body.

"Who goes there?" he called out.

Cass drew his horse to a halt. "A friend. Don't shoot. Name's Cass. Traveling to Watauga. Might you have a place for me to warm my bones on this cold night?"

Never lowering his gun, the man instructed him to tie his horse to the tether rope next to his own horse and come into the cabin. Before doing so, Cass took the bundle of deerskins from the horse and toted them over his shoulder into the warmth of the tiny abode. He'd made a mistake trusting that trader fellow early on in his journey, and he wasn't about to lose sight of these skins.

"What say your name was again?" the man asked as he came through the door.

"You can just call me Cass."

The man studied him a moment, then replied, "All right, then. My name's Greenlee. You can call me Hiram. Come inside before this danged wind blows us away."

Cass stepped into the cabin and was grateful for the warmth, although the wind had found holes in the chinks between the logs and whistled its way inside. He became aware of a figure silhouetted in front of the fireplace. A woman had her back to him, so he couldn't see her face, but her hair was long and plaited down her back, Indian style.

An iron pot hung above the fire, and Hiram Greenlee latched the door behind Cass and went to stir what was cooking in it. Whatever it was, it smelled heavenly to Cass, who hadn't eaten much except fish and venison in the past few months. Something about the scent reminded him of his childhood in his mother's small log cabin in Echoe.

"Won'tcha stash your bundle there in the corner and sit a bit?" Greenlee offered a chair by the fire. Reluctantly Cass placed the bundle in a corner where he could keep an eye on it.

Greenlee saw his look and laughed. "No worries, lad. I won't be stealin' your goods. I'm a trader myself. I know how hard it is to come by such skins. You alone in these woods?"

Cass had to weigh whether to trust this man, and yet he figured he had no good options. "Just me and my horse," he answered, taking a seat and casting a glance at the stewing kettle. Only then did he turn to see the face of the woman who'd remained silent since he'd entered the cabin. At first, he thought his eyes deceived him, or that it was a fancy of his imagination, but he thought he recognized those high cheekbones and long, straight nose. Her hair was almost solid white, and her ruddy skin was wizened and wrinkled.

"Quella?"

BIBLIOGRAPHY

Alderman, Pat, *The Overmountain Men*, Johnson City, TN: Overmountain Press, 1986.

Bartram, William, *Travels of William Bartram*, edited by Mark Van Doren. New York: Dover Publications, 1955.

Bassett, John Spencer, *The Regulators of North Carolina*, Trinity College, NC, 1894.

Conley, Robert J., *Cherokee Dragon*. Norman, OK: University of Oklahoma Press, 2000.

Dixon, Max, *The Wataugans*. Johnson City, TN: Overmountain Press, 1989.

Duncan, Barbara, collector and editor, *Living Stories of the Cherokee*. Chapel Hill, NC: The University of North Carolina Press, 1998.

Fink, Paul M., "Jacob Brown of Nolichucky." Tennessee Historical Quarterly, Vol. 1. No. 1, Sept. 1962.

Furbee, Mary R., *Wild Rose-Nancy Ward and the Cherokee Nation*. Greensboro, NC: Morgan Reynolds Publishers, Inc., 2002.

Lee, E. Lawrence, *Indian Wars in North Carolina*, 1663-1763. Raleigh, NC: Office of Archives & History, North Carolina Department of Cultural Resources, 2011.

Maas, John R., *The French & Indian War in North Carolina*. Charleston, SC: The History Press, 2013.

McCrumb, Sharyn, *Kings Mountain*, New York: Thomas Dunne Books, St. Martin's Press, 2013.

Mooney, James, *Myths of the Cherokee*. New York: Dover Publications, 1995. (Reprint of Government Printing Office edition, 1900.)

Morgan, Robert, *Boone, A Biography*, Chapel Hill, NC: Algonquin Books of Chapel Hill, 2008.

Ritchie, Fiona, and Doug Orr, *Wayfaring Strangers-The Musical Voyage from Scotland and Ulster to Appalachia*. Chapel Hill, NC: The University of North Carolina Press, 2014.

Shames, Susan P., *The Old Plantation-The Artist Revealed.* Williamsburg, VA: The Colonial Williamsburg Foundation, 2010.

Swann, Anne Landis, *The Other Side of the River.* Kearney, NE: Morris Publishing, 2010.

Swisher, James K., *The Revolutionary War in the Southern Back Country.* Gretna, LA: Pelican Publishing Company, 2008.

The Junior League of Charleston, Inc., *Charleston Receipts.* Memphis, TN: Starr Toof Cookbook Division, 1950.

Timberlake, Henry, *Memoirs.* Signal Mountain, TN: Mountain Press, 2001 (reprint of original work, 1762.)

Woodward, Grace Steele, *The Cherokees.* Norman, OK: University of Oklahoma Press, 1963.